KIOZHI

KIRENAI FATED MATES
BOOK SIX

TAMSIN LEY

Twin Leaf Press

Cover by The Book Brander

Paperback version
ISBN-13: 978-1-950027-66-8
Copyright © 2022 Twin Leaf Press
All rights reserved.

Twin Leaf Press
PO Box 672255
Chugiak, AK 99567

ACKNOWLEDGMENTS

Special thanks to Margaret K. and Cynthia I. for helping me name the fancy restaurant on board the ship - the *Amorous Starlove Solarium* (called ASS for short).

Dear reader,

Be sure to check out the glossary at the back if you are into that sort of thing. Plus there is a bonus section with descriptions of the alien races you may encounter in this series. Happy reading!

XOXO

Tamsin

KIOZHI

"You look like you could use a swig or ten of something strong," I say to Tazhio as we step onto the crowded observation deck.

This is the first night of the Intergalactic Dating Agency's inaugural cruise with human passengers, and the effervescent sensation of hundreds of emotions prickle against my empathic senses. The nebula shining through the dome overhead bathes everyone in an aurora of pastel colors, and a small band plays an upbeat Fogarian waltz while people on the dance floor spin and sway.

Tazhio has the worried look of an old man who's lost his way. He snags two glasses of Lensoran bubbly from a passing tray. "Got it covered."

He didn't want to be here tonight, but he's a good friend and agreed to be my *wingman*, a human term for one male who supports another during courting. Like me, he's Kirenai, but he's in his Hypawan form, which looks mostly human except for overly large eyes and very thick hair. As part of the crew, he wears a white uniform that stands out amidst the mostly black clothing worn by everyone else.

I smile, take a glass for myself, then turn my attention back to the humans. My human-style finery—a "tux", the tailor called it—fits my current human form perfectly; broad shoulders, tall straight spine, muscular legs ending on flat feet. The Intergalactic Dating Agency assured us this template is the most pleasing to human females. It took many cycles after Nanaia's passing, but I've re-trained my matrix to assume the shapes of other species, and can modify my features to please whichever woman I might find pleasure with this evening.

Many of the females stand in small clusters surrounded by male suitors from every race across the galaxy. The females have so many lovely shades of skin; deep brown, golden, and some who are as pale as starlight. The women all wear different fashions, from gauzy to svelte, though most seem to favor the color black, and the smells of so many perfumes are almost overwhelming.

A light-skinned female strides past me in a knee-length black dress with a cutout back panel that exposes the ridge of her spine. A unique hair clip with a spray of gems that look like stars holds her dark brown hair away from her face. I gaze after her appreciatively until a Kirenai following close on her heels with an enormous case in his arms glares at me, his aura radiating menace.

I understand immediately. It was that way with Nanaia when we met, an all-consuming desire that couldn't be ignored. The devastating accident that took her from me sent me into a depression that ruled my life for many cycles.

I jerk my attention away from that particular female—I won't interfere with someone finding a mate. I'm not here to replace Nanaia—that would be impossible. Kirenai mate for life, and finding my true mate had been a one-in-a-million chance, anyway. But my body still has needs, and I can afford to treat any female who wishes to be with me like a princess.

My attention stops on a pretty brunette talking to several other women. Her hair is piled on top of her head, cascading down in a mass of curls. Her lips have been painted with a glistening red substance that reminds me of fruit. A slit in her long black dress exposes a length of golden thigh I'd love to explore further.

I step forward, running my gaze up and down her curves. "Hello, ma'am."

The woman turns to me with an assessing glance, eyes narrowed. "Ma'am? Do I look like a ma'am?"

The IDA told us we should use the term in polite human conversation. Apparently, they were wrong. "My apologies. I was informed the title was honorific. What shall I call you?"

"I'm Amanda, and this is Genevieve and Flora." She gestures toward a tall blonde and a petite brunette. They nod in greeting.

"I'm Kiozhi." I take her hand, turning her palm up to brush a kiss across her skin. My *Iki'i* senses the giddy thrill racing through her at my touch, yet she firmly pulls her hand free of my grip. I don't allow this to stop me—this is most likely why the literature about humans suggests bringing a wingman while courting. "This is my friend, Tazhio. As you can see, he's Kirenai too."

Tazhio is looking out at the crowd, not paying attention to the women at all. I elbow him and he jerks his gaze back to Amanda. "Oh, yes, greetings."

The women all giggle and nod appreciatively at him. I frown. The guidebook said nothing about the wingman competing for female attention. Perhaps I shouldn't have brought him after all.

"So," the other brunette drawls, "what are you two looking for in a woman?"

I seize the opportunity to remove Tazhio from consideration. "Tazhio's not allowed to date the passengers. But I would be happy to explore a night of pleasure with you."

She places a finger against her chin thoughtfully and looks me up and down again. "Oh, I bet you would," she says, her voice heavy with sarcasm. "But we're here looking for relationships, not one-night stands."

I blink, not fully understanding her terminology. She seems to interpret my confusion as confirmation of her judgement and turns away. *Kuzara.* Finding companionship among these humans isn't going to be as quick and easy as I imagined.

I turn to complain to Tazhio but find he's abandoned me, disappeared somewhere into the crowd. I sigh. So much for my wingman.

On the dance floor, several beautiful women are moving to the music, laughing, flirting with their partners. I move forward to watch. Each female is divine in her own way, though I can't help comparing each one to my Nanaia and have to determinedly redirect my thoughts. I divert myself by imagining what it might be like to entwine myself with one of these females, to feel her body pressed against mine, our tongues dancing together in passion. Though my mate is gone, my sex drive is not, and providing pleasure gives me joy and helps keep my lingering depression at bay.

A laugh catches my attention. It reminds me of a clear waterfall chiming against the crystal cliffs on my home planet of Alkavar III. *Who is that?* A longing rises through me. I want to be the one making her laugh.

Intrigued, I follow the sound and discover a female with ivory skin and the most delightful shade of hair I've ever encountered—a light red-gold that reminds me of a sunset. She's twirling across the dance floor in the arms of a Kirenai my *Iki'i* doesn't recognize. Her short black dress is covered in small scales that catch the light with pearly iridescence. The glimmer accentuates her curves in a way that makes my heart pound faster.

She spins past me, brilliant green eyes connecting with mine for an instant. My mating shaft stirs, a long-forgotten ache flaring low in my belly. I stumble back in confusion. I haven't felt this sensation since Nanaia died.

The female tosses her hair and looks away, an amused grin on her face as the other male guides her across the dance floor. Normally, I'd approach her without hesitation, but I need to understand what's happening first. This sensation can't be normal.

I push through the crowd to keep up with her, trying to remain a mere a shadow in the distance. My breathing quickens as I watch her hips sway. I feel like a youth again, eager and impulsive. She's mine, I know it. I must win her away from this other male.

2

SUZANNE

$\mathcal{I}$ tip my head back and laugh as I spin across the dance floor in the arms of yet another tall blue alien. So far, I've danced with at least six Kirenai, a short, hairy alien called a Fogarian, and a tall, stone-like beast of a man with wings and horns. After seventeen years trapped in a co-dependent marriage, I'm finally free, and I made a promise to myself that I wouldn't dance with the same guy twice—though telling the uniformly good-looking blue aliens apart might be a challenge. I haven't had this much fun since before I got knocked up in high school, and now that the kids are grown and gone, I'm determined to make the most of this two-week singles' cruise through space.

The song ends, and I snag a glass of whatever this stuff is that passes for alien champagne from a passing server's tray. I pull my arm free of my dance partner's. "Thank you for the dance. I need to catch my breath."

He opens his mouth to respond, but I duck behind a couple doing a flailing approximation of swing dancing and move away. The room is filled with all sorts of aliens, from handsome blue Kirenai with action figure bodies to short, frail-looking Area 51 beings with gray-green skin and huge dark eyes.

Overhead, multicolored ribbons of light speckled with thousands of glittering stars illuminate the domed ceiling. Sipping the bubbly, fruity drink and smiling at every hot alien who glances my direction, I move back toward where I left my sisters at the edge of the dance floor. I feel self-conscious in my silky black cocktail dress with iridescent sequins but force myself to have positive thoughts about being sexy and keep my chin high.

All around me is laughter and talking in a hundred different languages. I'm still wrapping my head around the fact I can understand them all—alien and human alike—thanks to a translator implant I get to keep when the trip is over. Maybe I can use it to land a job as a corporate translator when I get back to Earth. Wouldn't that be something?

I pass by a hulking gray dude with wings, horns, and a tail who gives me a once-over before breaking into a sharp-toothed grin. His bod is rock-solid, though his features are a bit too chiseled for my taste, and he carries himself like a conceited asshole. It's that last part that I turn away from. I've had enough of men who think they're God's gift to women—my husband used me to get through med school, then divorced me for a hot young blonde he was having an affair with.

Fucking bastard.

I dodge another alien who's looking at me with a proprietary gaze and search for my sisters. I want to see if they're having fun too. Lifting my chin, I locate Jennifer fiddling with her telescope at one edge of the observation deck. She's insisting on using this trip to gather astronomy data for her doctoral thesis and is somehow successfully ignoring the constant stream of alien men asking her to dance. It probably helps that the tall, bald Kirenai who's been hauling her equipment around glares daggers at anyone who comes near.

I'd prefer not to be dragged into one of my brainy sister's dissertations about random star systems, so I keep looking. I spot Tamara's copper curls among the crowd. She's heading to the dance floor with an alien who looks like a dwarf who's been dipped in red paint. *Good for her.* She's usually so shy, I'm glad to see she's having fun.

That only leaves our baby sister, Bethany. I know just where to look for her—near the kitchen, stalking an alien chef she wants to host on her cooking show.

Spotting her next to the service doors where tables are laden with appetizer trays, I swoop over and take her hand. "God, I'm having such a good time. Take a break and dance with me."

"Stop, Suzanne." She yanks her hand away, planting it back on the hip of her deep wine-colored cocktail dress. "There's a Nebula Chef on board, and I'm waiting to speak with him. I wish they'd just let me go talk to him in the kitchen."

I sigh. Just like Jennifer, Bethany has a one-track mind when it comes to her career. I examine the alien appetizers on a nearby table and pick up something that looks exactly like a small red penis. "Maybe they're not letting you in the kitchen because they don't want you to find out their alien dicks aren't fresh." I waggle my eyebrows suggestively.

One of the small Area 51-looking servers stumbles slightly, obviously overhearing me. I flash him a naughty grin, sure his cheeks turn pink underneath all that gray skin before he turns and scurries away.

"Quit joking around. This is serious." Bethany scowls, snatching the food out of my hand and taking an aggressive bite. She waves the other half in my face. "You're the only one who insisted this trip was all about meeting hot aliens. Dance with one of them." She gestures toward a nearby Kirenai.

Most of the blue aliens look similar, but there's something about this one that makes my engine rev. Perhaps it's the magnetism of his midnight dark eyes. I'm not sure if I've danced with him before, but he's hot enough I might consider a second turn around the dance floor, promise to myself be damned.

He moves forward and holds out a hand. "I noticed you from across the room." His rumbling voice cuts below the music. Ok, I know I haven't danced with him because I would've remembered that voice. "My name's Kiozhi. Would you care to dance?"

"Sure." I shrug, trying not to appear eager as I start past him toward the dance floor.

He stops me with an arm around my waist. Pulling me closer, he starts to sway to the music. Maybe it's the slightly crooked way he smiles, or the subtle, almost chocolaty scent of his cologne, but I find myself looping my arms around his neck. "Something wrong with the dance floor?"

Guiding me in time to the music, he leans close to my ear. "There are too many people there. I want you all to myself."

Oh, boy. That deep voice really makes my girly parts flutter. The TV shows on Earth make Kirenai out to be mind-bogglingly exceptional lovers, which I always assumed must be fiction. Now's my chance to find out for real.

I've never had a one-night stand, but I'm starting to think tonight is the night. It's a big step for me. *You are allowed to have fun.* I repeat the self-talk my therapist encouraged me to use.

Tilting my head back, I meet his gaze. "That's hard to do in a room full of people."

He pulls me tighter against him. Heat pools between my legs as I feel the throbbing length now trapped between our bodies. "Yes, very hard."

I don't even recall his name, but I don't care. I close the distance between our lips. His arms fold around me like a cloak as his kiss ravages my mouth. His fingers toy with the hair at the base of my neck, sending shivers down my spine. I wrap both arms around his ribs and let my hands play up and down the broad muscles of his back. Our tongues tangle until I've lost all sense of space and time.

I'm panting with desire and my nipples ache inside my dress by the time he pauses. I want him to touch me all over, skin to skin. Voice raspy with need, I ask, "Should we take this back to your room or mine?"

3

KIOZHI

The moment the female—Suzanne, I heard her sister call her—presses her lips against mine, fire ignites my blood. I still find it impossible that I've discovered another mate, but there is no denying the surge of my mating shaft or the surety in my heart. I pull her tightly against me and let myself revel in our connection. Never did I expect to feel this way a second time.

She takes my hand and hurries us toward the lift. I let her lead, still in shock from my roiling sensations. As the lift descends, she faces me again, both hands around my neck, nipples hardened to points I can feel even through our clothing. Her tongue invades my mouth, and I open for her, letting her take all she desires. She's sweet and intoxicating, our tongues engaging in a battle neither of us can win nor lose.

By the time we reach her room, she has already removed my tie and opened my shirt to run her hands over my pecs and abs. I don't know how much longer I can wait to bury myself in her heat. But I recall reading that humans prefer a slow courtship, and I want Suzanne to treasure our bonding moment. We'll have hundreds of cycles together once I claim her, so I don't need to rush this now.

The cabin door has barely spiraled shut before she reaches behind her and opens the back of her dress, letting the silk folds slide into a puddle around her ankles. Her body is magnificent, clad in nothing but a thin triangle of cloth covering her sex. I want to taste her full, rosy nipples. Her hips are wide and curvy, and her sunset hair curls wildly around her shoulders.

"*Oritsu*," I breathe. "You are magnificent."

She grins wickedly and uses both hands to shove my jacket and shirt off my shoulders.

I unfasten the front of my pants, relief washing through me as my cock is allowed to spring free. Then I firmly push her back onto the mattress and kneel on the edge of the bed so I can look at her. I'm doing my best to increase the anticipation, but it's becoming difficult to restrain myself.

Her eyes are dark, and she raises both arms to welcome me. "Come here."

I can't resist. Lowering myself against her softness, I kiss her again, letting one hand roam the bounty of her curves. She moans when my fingers slide between her legs. Her heat is like lava through her panties.

"Please," she begs, flexing her hips toward my touch.

I don't need to be asked twice. Ripping her panties from her body, I slide a finger inside her. She moans louder, and my *Iki'i* revels in the growing frenzy of her pleasure. A certain spot inside her seems to drive her wild, so I focus pressure there, finding the rhythm that pleases her most.

When I press my thumb to her clit, her head thrashes back and forth. She's lost to sensation, no longer capable of returning my kisses. I grin and nibble my way down her neck until I reach her breasts, licking and sucking. She grips the covers on either side of her, writhing and gasping, her inner walls fluttering on the verge of release.

"Come for me," I say.

My beautiful Suzanne complies, her body arching up from the mattress as her channel convulses around my fingers.

When her shuddering subsides, I withdraw my finger and feather her face with kisses. She's flushed and panting, her satisfaction like a salve on my *Iki'i*.

After a moment, she regains enough strength to turn her lips to mine, and our tongues resume their dance. Her delicate hands travels down my rib cage to my waist, and one slides between us to find my primary shaft. I groan as her fingers close around it. Her thumb rolls over the head, spreading slick pre-cum in a small circular motion that almost makes me lose control.

She murmurs into my mouth, "I want you inside me."

I'm ready too. More than ready. But I know if I take her from the front, there will be no controlling my mating shaft. I wouldn't be able to stop myself from claiming her here and now, and I want to give her the courting she deserves before we seal our bond. Gripping her hips, I roll her onto her stomach, then pull her back so she's resting on her knees.

I can't resist the urge to look at the puckered hole of her ass, so I spread her cheeks gently and let my thumb press against her tightness. She's slick there from the juices drenching her pussy, and she gasps and tightens as I press more firmly without quite entering.

"This is for later," I growl before bending down to nip her ass cheek.

Then I position myself behind her. She opens her legs wider when I settle between them, and I grasp her hips to hold her still. The tip of my primary shaft presses into her channel, and she exhales with a low moan.

She's so wet, I have no trouble sliding my length inside her, adjusting my shape and size to fill her completely. My mating shaft, thwarted from entering her ass, glides across her clit.

I shudder at the stimulation, rocking my hips back and forth a few times. It won't be enough to provide the double ejaculation I crave, but it feels good, especially when she arches her back to accept each deep thrust. I can feel her tightening around me and know she's close.

Pistoning forward, I drive into her again and again until she explodes, straining back against me. She cries out, her juices flowing in heated rivulets over my balls.

I can't stop myself. "Suzanne," I hiss her name, every muscle in my body tightening as my release shoots deep inside her.

She moans, spasms of release still rolling through her, milking me of everything I have. I pulse and throb, trapped in her body's tight embrace. All I can hear is the sound of my breathing, the beat of my heart, the rush of blood in my ears. All I can smell is the sweet scent of her pleasure.

When I finally return to my senses, I take a moment to enjoy the perfect sway of her back. Her hands loosely clutch the bedsheets, and her pale red-gold hair is plastered to her cheek with sweat. She's the most phenomenal sight I've ever seen. *My mate.* I can only imagine what pleasures our actual bonding will bring.

With her lovely, heart-shaped ass still securely against my hips and my shaft still inside her body, I roll us over and wrap my arm around her, breathing in the floral perfume of her hair.

"That was incredible," she whispers, her ribs rising and falling with breath.

I nibble her ear, loving the way she shudders and snuggles closer. "That was only the beginning, my *kikajiru.*"

4

SUZANNE

I wake feeling boneless and sated; the propaganda about Kirenai lovers is not an exaggeration. I never even learned my alien lover's name, but I'm still high on the aftermath of our night together hours after he left my cabin. He worshipped every inch of my body at least twice, and I lost count of the number of times I climaxed.

I stretch languidly between the soft sheets and let my gaze wander around the room. It looks like almost any other hotel room, with a bed, vanity, and chest of drawers. The walls are a soft gray, and the rest of the room is decorated in pearl fixtures with deep purple accents. Not my favorite colors, but elegant and sensual. The sheets still smell like our lovemaking, and I'm filled with a twinge of longing. "Get it together,

Suzanne," I mutter to myself. "He's supposed to be just another notch in your lipstick case."

My attention snags on a brilliant green and orange flower arrangement on my vanity. *Where did that come from?* The steward must've delivered it while I was asleep. I glance toward the closed door, feeling a bit creeped out, but these are aliens, so I guess they might not understand etiquette when it comes to privacy. A card pokes from the center of the bouquet.

I fling the sheets aside and stand, pulling on the fluffy white bath robe provided with the room. The bouquet smells like bergamot and peppermint, and the shapes of the blooms are fascinating, like a cross between a bird of paradise and sea holly. I reach for the card and flip it over. *Thank you for the extraordinary evening. Let's meet for lunch on the observation deck. I look forward to furthering our acquaintance. Sincerely, Kiozhi.*

Excitement and terror wage war within my chest. I'm flattered he liked me enough to want more, but I'm not here to latch onto the first guy I meet. I know myself too well; if I accept the invitation, I won't so much as glance at another guy for the rest of the cruise.

"At least I know his name now," I mutter, tossing the card on the bed. Heading to the shower, I wash off all traces of the previous night before getting dressed to join my sisters for lunch.

Bethany wants to try one of the little specialty restaurants, so we head below deck and wind our way through the halls to the nearest lift. The *Romantasy* is shaped like a donut with multiple levels, and we could walk for hours without recrossing our path, but every lift has a button that takes us directly where we want to go. I have no idea how it works, but it's pretty cool.

The restaurant is filled with the din of other guests, a chorus of voices that rise and fall in pitch and volume. Legless tables hang from the ceiling by large cables, and the floor is tiled in red and black geometric shapes. Surprisingly, the air smells of cinnamon and vanilla—not alien at all—as we take our seats.

Bethany chatters about her upcoming birthday and how she's convinced one of the cruise chefs to make her a special cake as a demo for her new cooking show. "I booked this entire restaurant for the party," she says gesturing to our surroundings. "I'll film a demo my producers can't resist. Go big or go home, right?"

"I don't know, Bethany," Jennifer shakes her head. "Are you sure you should put all your eggs in one basket like this? I mean, you haven't even met him."

"It's fine! I'm not worried about the food—this guy's a Nebula Chef. Plus, he's Kirenai, so he'll look hot for the camera." She taps a finger against her lips. "But I'll ask him create a face with character. I don't want him to look like the generic Ken dolls around here." Bethany turns to look at me. "Speaking of Ken dolls, how was your night? What do these aliens look like under their clothes?"

"He definitely wasn't a neutered doll," I say. My sisters giggle appreciatively, and I smirk. Leaning in close, I fill them in on the details. "He sent me flowers and a thank you note this morning. I may have to try one of those guys with horns and wings next to get Kiozhi out of my system."

Even as I say it, an uncomfortable feeling roils in the pit of my stomach. I may not be cut out for this bed-hopping thing. But at least I did it once, and it was a hell of a ride. Even if I don't take another lover for the rest of the trip, I can honestly say I had fun.

When we finish eating, I head back to my cabin. A ribbon-wrapped box of chocolates waits on the end of my bed. *Another gift from Kiozhi?* I pull the note off the box and turn it over. Carefully drawn calligraphy sweeps over the thick card stock.

My sweet Suzanne, the note begins. *I'm sorry we missed each other at lunch today. Please accept my invitation to dinner this evening at a private booth in the Amorous Starlove Solarium. I'll be at your cabin at eight to escort you. With sincere affection, Kiozhi.*

The Amorous Starlove Solarium—ASS for short, which put me and my sisters in stitches when the cruise director first introduced it—is the most expensive restaurant on the ship, the only dining that isn't included in the cruise package. Hands trembling, I shove the card back under the ribbon. *Bethany is going to kill me for refusing.* But I can't accept, no matter how elite the invitation.

I summon a ship's steward and ask him to return the chocolates.

The small gray alien who arrives at my door gazes longingly at the box and licks his lips. "These are exotic delicacies," he says, slowly blinking his large eyes like Puss in Boots. "Would you like a credit at the gift shop?"

He looks so pitiful and hungry, I'm tempted to tell him he can have the candy. Except I can't, because I need to be sure Kiozhi knows I returned his gift. "No, thank you. I need you to refund the purchaser's account. His name's on the card."

The steward nods, and I close the door. I really hope Kiozhi takes the hint now, because this cruise is supposed to be the "Hot Girl Summer" I never had. My kids are grown and out on their own, I'll have an apartment to myself for the first time in my life, and I've already signed up for classes to get my horticulture degree. I'm still young enough to start over, and that's exactly what I'm going to do.

No way am I falling for the first guy I take to my bed, no matter how amazing Kiozhi looks or how good he makes me feel.

KIOZHI

The glass of something called whiskey sitting in front of me smells warm and slightly spicy. It burns pleasantly when it goes down. Right after I left Suzanne's cabin, I looked up everything I could about her, then re-read the IDA's information packet about humans, absorbing everything I can about my mate's culture. The packet indicated human females prefer knowledgeable males, so I'm sampling everything on board related to Earth so I don't look like a fool when I see Suzanne again.

Right now, I'm sitting in the ship's forward lounge—a circular area with lots of metal and glass, from the shelves holding bottles of imported Earth liquor to the gleaming metal stools set around high top glass tables. To either side of me at the bar, clusters of unattached males stare longingly at the couples scattered about the room. There are fewer females than males on this cruise, and only a lucky few will return home with mates.

I smugly take another sip of whiskey and continue surveying the shelves of bottles. Soon I'll also be receiving envious stares from unmated males. I still can't fathom my fortune in finding Suzanne; second mates are beyond rare. I even doubted my senses at first, but our physical intimacy last night made me more than certain it's true—my *Iki'i* can't lie. But I also need to respect the human custom of taking things slow. Human females enjoy what they call an engagement period, so I'm going to use our time on board the ship to make sure she knows just how precious she is.

My Integrated Circuit Chip pings, and I tap my arm to bring up the ICC interface. I scowl when I see it's a return receipt from the gift shop. I was very specific with my instructions. Why are they refunding my money? When I scroll down, my heart seizes in my chest. *Suzanne rejected my gift?*

I glance around, no longer smug at the sight of so many couples staring lovingly into each other's eyes. At a table across the room, a female holds up one hand, beaming at a gem-studded ring. The male across from her is grinning like a fool, their happiness strong enough to make every nearby Kirenai smile too.

I don't smile. I can't. The information packet said flowers and chocolate are standard exchanges humans use to communicate affection. Suzanne didn't reject the flowers. Is she a rare female who doesn't like chocolate?

Confidence returning, I allow myself to smile. *My mate is special.* I'll have to try harder to learn what she likes. Dinner tonight will help me understand her preferences in food. And perhaps I should also look into some jewelry.

Downing the remainder of my drink, I head to the gift shop to peruse the gemstones on board. I'll present her with a lavish bauble when I see her at dinner tonight.

5

SUZANNE

I step out of my cabin and nearly bump into my sister Jennifer. Her usual, massive blue porter stands a few steps behind her holding her astronomy case. She's in denim shorts and a black t-shirt filled with stars and the words *I need my space*. As always, she has her beat-up messenger bag hooked over one shoulder.

I raise an eyebrow. "Are you bringing that thing to karaoke?"

"No," she scowls. "The karaoke bar doesn't have any viewing portals. I'm on my way to drop this stuff off at my cabin first. These social evenings are such a waste of time."

"Cut loose and have some fun," I say, sliding a glance toward her porter. I swear he looks more like Vin

Diesel every day, and I know my sister has a thing for the hunky actor. "It's just for a few hours."

"Hours I could use in far more productive ways." She waves a hand and tromps by me and unlocks her cabin. "You guys go on without me. I'll meet you there."

I shrug and knock on Tamara's door. I'm waiting for her to answer when I hear my name from down the hall. A handsome blue Kirenai in a tuxedo strides in my direction. Though he looks the same as most other Kirenai on board, I know in my heart it's Kiozhi. I gulp, heart fluttering like an army of butterflies.

"Shit," I mutter, wondering if it's too late to pretend I didn't see him and go back to my cabin.

Kiozhi comes to a stop next to me, his warm, masculine scent taking me back to the bliss of last night. Voice low and intimate, he says, "Suzanne, you look absolutely stunning."

My entire body heats at the compliment. I'm not usually a dressy person, but I bought all new clothes for this trip. Tonight I'm wearing a gold sequined tank top, Spanx tuxedo leggings, and black stiletto sandals, ready for the promised karaoke on tonight's social calendar. After years of keeping my strawberry blonde hair tucked up and away from my face, it now hangs loose around my bare shoulders.

I smile tightly, not quite looking at Kiozhi. My ex would always qualify his praise with something backhanded, and I can't help the instinct to brace myself for the other shoe to drop. Staring at my sister's door, I opt for a simple, "Thank you."

"Are you ready for dinner?" Kiozhi holds out an elbow as if expecting me to take it. "Or would you prefer drinks first?"

Relief floods through me as the door spirals open, revealing Tamara. Her gray eyes widen, taking in Kiozhi's well-cut figure. "Oh."

I push past her into the room. "Sorry, Kiozhi. I have other plans tonight. Thanks for the invitation, though."

I refuse to turn around until I hear the door spiral closed again.

"Is that your stalker?" Our youngest sister, Bethany, asks from inside the room. She's standing in front of a full-length mirror next to the bed, a curling iron in one hand. Her elegant silver cocktail dress is slit up one side, nearly to her hip. I always wished I had a body like my baby sister's. I don't know how she can stay so fit when she's always sampling food for her cooking show.

"Hush." I sit on the end of the bed next to Tamara's chihuahua, Beanie, who is happily chewing a stuffed animal. "He might be listening."

Bethany goes back to curling her auburn hair. "So? Sometimes you have to hurt someone's feelings to get them to take a hint."

I sigh. I'm not usually a fan of my baby sister's brashness, but she has a point. Yet the thought of hurting Kiozhi makes my insides feel all squiggly and uncomfortable.

Tamara picks up her dog so she can sit next to me. She's dressed in a green peekaboo blouse and black leggings that are quickly covered with dog hair. "I bet he'll be at karaoke tonight."

"He'll take the hint soon," I say. "I'm sure he'll find another woman for his affections at the party." That would be the easiest solution. So why is my stomach tight at the thought of seeing him with someone else?

"Aren't you the one always telling us to be direct about what we want?" asks Bethany, a snide smirk on her lips.

I stick my tongue out at her. "Yes. I'll be direct the next time I see him." At least, I hope I will. The memory of his hands on my body, the warm, almost chocolaty scent of his skin, the feathery kisses as we enjoyed the afterglow make it difficult to be firm in my rejection. I shake off my longing. "Everyone ready to go?"

We head to the party, taking the lift to another of the *Romantasy's* many decks and following the corridor toward where I can hear someone belting out the lyrics to "Faith" by George Michael. Inside the darkened bar, a disco ball flashes multi-colored lights over the crowd. Aliens of all shapes and sizes cluster around gyrating human women.

The only requirement that came with our free cruise tickets is that we attend nightly social events with the aliens. No problem. Each alien is hunkier than the last, depending on your taste in men. I'm partial to the somewhat generic GQ look most of the Kirenai seem to have adopted, and yet the moment I spot Kiozhi at the bar, every other guy might as well be hamburger. He's still in his tailored tux, his blue hair in a stylishly tousled French crop I vividly remember clutching while his face was between my legs.

Dammit. What is wrong with me? He has no right to consume my thoughts like this. I must have sex on the brain because I had such a long dry spell after my divorce. Yes, that's it. Any of these hot guys would make me feel the same way.

Beside me, Tamara stands on her tiptoes, searching the crowd. "Do you see him?"

I can barely hear her over the gravelly voice of a winged alien attempting to sing something that reminds me of a sea shanty, but I know she's looking for her hot shuttle pilot. I glance around the teeming crowd, nearly blinded by the flashing lights. Leaning close, I shout. "Not yet, but let's keep looking!"

Bethany taps my arm and gestures toward a row of tables where a Kirenai in a chef's hat has his back to us. "I think I see my chef. I'll be over there."

I nod at her and spare another glance toward Kiozhi. He's chatting with a waif-like woman with straight black hair that hangs well below the short hem of her red cocktail dress. Her stilettos are impossibly high, and the muscles of her perfectly shaped legs gleam in the disco lights.

Jealousy actually lodges in my throat. I swallow it down. *What the hell is wrong with me?* This is not at all what I should feel. I should be relieved he's found another woman who's happy to be the focus of his attention.

My loyalty issues are getting out of hand. I need to distract myself, fast. I latch on to the nearest blue alien and ask him to sing with me.

His dark eyes light eagerly, and he puts an arm around my shoulders. "I have just the song for us."

As he leads me toward the stage, I resist the urge to shrug off his arm. His skin feels tacky and overly warm against mine.

We climb onto the short platform and the opening notes to "I Got You Babe" by Sonny and Cher start to play. I clumsily follow the words on the screen, while my partner seems to have this song well-rehearsed, replicating Sonny's tenor notes perfectly and making a point of grabbing my hand every time the main chorus repeats.

I try my best to keep my focus on Tamara in the audience, but my attention wanders to the bar where Kiozhi stands with his arms crossed. I can't tell if he's hurt or angry. Do I care? My head says no, but there's an uncomfortable twinge in my chest. *Dammit, do not let yourself fall for puppy dog eyes.* Yes, that one night was great, but it was only one night. This guy singing with me could be great too.

To prove it, I smile at my duet partner and loop my arm through his as we step off the stage to mild applause. "Buy me a drink?"

"It would be my pleasure." Unfortunately, he guides me straight to the bar where Kiozhi is standing. I position myself with my back to Kiozhi as the bartender hands me my drink—a flowery green thing that's overly sweet. I'm pretty sure my karaoke partner just told me his name, but I can't seem to focus. I swear I can feel Kiozhi's stare on the back of my neck.

After a few moments of nodding at small talk, I can't take it anymore. I glance over my shoulder.

Kiozhi is gone.

I look around the bar but can't find him. Did he finally give up on me? I should be glad, but my hands are shaking and my heart races. I set my barely touched drink on the bar. "I'm not feeling very well," I say. "I'm going to retire. Thank you for the song."

"But wait, you—"

I dart for the door without waiting for him to finish. Once I'm safely in my room, I text my sisters that I left the party. Then I flop back on the bed where Kiozhi and I made love not all that long ago. I run both palms over the coverlet and sigh, squeezing my eyes shut at my mixed emotions.

I never expected my quest for freedom to feel this awful.

6

KIOZHI

I lean back in the co-pilot seat and look around the sparse shuttle cockpit. The view screen dominating the front wall shows the *Romantasy's* shuttle bay doors open to the stars, the golden glimmer of the atmospheric force shield flickering now and then. Through the open portal to the rear of the compartment I can hear the low voices of guests boarding the shuttle.

I pivot my chair to face Tazhio in the pilot seat. "Why am I here again?"

"An excursion to the Singing Planet is guaranteed to take your mind off your other problems." Tazhio keeps his attention on the control panel, prepping for our upcoming flight. "You'll love it, I promise."

I make a doubtful sound at the back of my throat. Tazhio's always working, always able to keep his mind off his troubles. Not for the first time, I envy him. All I can think about is Suzanne's amazing voice as she sang last night, her promises of love directed at someone other than myself. I really need to find something else to focus on. "Is there something I can do to help?"

He barely glances at me. "Not unless you want to calculate shield modulation for friction induced plasma ionization."

"Pretty sure I skipped that class in school," I say wryly.

He chuckles, then abruptly silences. His alertness triggers my *Iki'i*, and I turn toward the sound of voices coming from outside the cockpit.

"Thank you, no." A woman's soft voice reaches me. "I'm with my sisters."

A gravelly voice replies, "We can make room for them..."

I stop listening at that point, conscious of my friend's reaction and the roiling jealousy now bombarding my *Iki'i*. I'm not the only one trying to distract myself from female interactions. One of the humans on board has gained his attention too, but he's not allowed to pursue her; the crew isn't allowed to look for mates among the guests. But finding a mate is so rare, I think he's being an idiot not to act, consequences be damned.

"Is that her?" I ask.

"Yes," he says, his voice raspy.

"You need to go see her," I say. "At least let me live vicariously through you. Go!"

"Are you trying to make me lose my job?" he says through gritted teeth. "You know my contract prohibits me from pursuing a mate among the guests."

"*Kuzara.*" I fling my hands up in exasperation. "Just say you're checking on the welfare of your passengers. If you get fired, I'll hire you as my private shuttle pilot."

He scowls. "I don't want your charity."

Yet he stands and moves toward the door as if unable to help himself. Moments later, he returns with a copper-haired female. I recognize her. She's one of Suzanne's sisters. *If she's on this tour, maybe Suzanne is too.*

I shoot to my feet. "Aren't you one of the Bloom sisters?"

She nods, glancing around the cockpit. "I don't mean to intrude…"

"Nonsense." I gesture toward the chair I just vacated. "I'm more than happy to exchange seats."

Before she can speak again, I squeeze past her into the passenger area, scanning the banks of plush red seats for Suzanne's familiar red-gold hair and pale skin. She's seated near the back, and the seat paired next to hers is empty. Grinning, I stride down the aisle toward her.

Her green eyes meet mine and a pretty flush rises to her cheeks. My *Iki'i* senses her attraction and draws me forward like a magnet.

Taking the seat adjoining hers, I lean over the shared armrest and give her a wink. "I hope you don't mind, but your sister traded seats with me."

Suzanne turns her shoulder away from me and crosses her arms. "I absolutely do—"

A voice over the intercom interrupts the rest of her words. "We've closed the hatch and are preparing to depart. Please remain seated until we clear the docking bay doors."

I give Suzanne a sly grin. "Guess you're stuck with me this time." I'm not going to let her push me away again. We have an entire excursion to spend together, and I plan to make the most of it.

"Oh, goodie," she mutters, still staring out the viewport.

The shuttle shivers momentarily as it lifts from the flight deck, then sails smoothly between the *Romantasy's* bay doors. Tazhio's an excellent pilot, and I bet he's pulling out all the stops to show off for his lady. I just need to find a way to do the same.

Keeping my voice low and intimate, I say, "I'm sorry you don't enjoy chocolate."

"Who says I don't like chocolate?" She glares at me from the corner of her eye.

"You returned my gift."

"I was trying to make a point," she says, exasperation clear in her tone.

"What point?" I ask.

She turns to look directly at me. "I'm not interested in you, Kiozhi. Stop stalking me."

Confusion fills me. Why is she lying? She can't hide her attraction to me. My *Iki'i* knows she feels it, the same way I know she gets aroused when I deepen my voice. Perhaps this is part of the human courting game. I make the decision not to back down. Looking directly into her amazing green eyes, I state, "No."

"Wh-what?" Her eyes widen, and surprise flickers across my *Iki'i*.

"I'm not stalking you," I clarify. "I'm courting you. I've been told human females enjoy this. Tell me what you want, and I will provide it."

"Never again." She crosses her arms and stares straight ahead.

I don't know what I'm supposed to do when my *Iki'i* is sensing one thing, and her words are telling me another. I glance at the Kirenai male across from me. He's leaning over the lap of another Bloom sister—Jennifer, I believe she's called. They seem to be having an intimate moment of attraction as she smiles at him, her fingertips lightly pressed to his arm.

I'm pretty sure he and I have met a few times at parties, though not in our current forms. He looks human, but much broader than the template the IDA provided, and he's completely bald. I assume that's in direct response to Jennifer's unspoken preferences. If so, it means he's been able to spend extensive time with her. A flicker of jealousy rises in me that he's had better luck. *Perhaps he can offer me advice.*

"Hey," I call to him. "You're Nazhin, the owner of Demod Industries, right?"

He stares at me. "Why would the owner of a corporation need to work as a porter?"

His words aren't exactly a lie, but I definitely get the sense he wants me to shut up. I glance toward Jennifer. Does he not want her to know who he is? But why? He's almost as wealthy as I am. Perhaps he's having difficulty courting too. Yet if Jennifer's current responses to him are any indication, he's doing something right. I'll have to ask him about his tactics later. For now, I'll let him continue his disguise.

"My mistake." I recline in my seat and wave a dismissive hand. "Back to your portering or whatever." Then a thought occurs to me. I lean closer to Suzanne. "Do humans have something against rich guys? Is that why you keep rejecting me?"

"Could you be more full of yourself?" she snaps before focusing her attention on her sister and Nazhin once more.

Kuzara. Will I ever get a straight answer out of her?

"What's Demod Industries?" Jennifer asks.

"A company that designs high-end sensor equipment," Nazhin supplies. "I believe they're currently the largest manufacturer in the galaxy."

Interest sparks in Jennifer's eyes. "Like astronomy equipment?"

"Certainly," he says. "But I'm afraid humans are banned from purchasing advanced technology until your planet is no longer on probation."

Suzanne drums her fingertips against her thigh, eyes narrowed on Nazhin's face. Suspicion pulses off her, and I get the sense she's going to call him out at any moment. If she blows his cover, it will be my fault, and

I don't want that. I smile broadly and lean forward, trying to draw their attention. "I could probably smuggle you a few things."

"Really?" Jennifer grins, eyes full of excitement.

An idea blinks like casino lights in my mind. *Can I sweet talk Jennifer into putting in a good word with her sister?* "Of course." I shrug nonchalantly. "Just tell me what you need."

Suzanne rolls her eyes. "Don't encourage him."

Jennifer ignores her. "Could you get me a sensor that can calculate the Roche limit of a planetary body?"

I have no idea what any of the words she just said even mean, but I say, "I'll ask my contact once we get back to the *Romantasy.*" I turn to face Suzanne. "Is there anything I can get you?"

Just then, multi-colored light fills the cabin, and everyone turns toward the viewport. Outside, a braided tangle of brilliant pink, green, and yellow light flows against a backdrop of velvet-black space.

"This is your captain." Tazhio's voice comes over the speakers as the seat cushion softens beneath me. "I've engaged the cabin's safety features. It's normal to encounter some turbulence during this excursion, so please sit back and enjoy the galactic symphony."

Golden streamers of light float through the cabin, followed by a high, sweet note I can feel to the depths of my matrix. The lights are amazing, but I'm more enraptured by Suzanne's soft gasps of wonder. She made such noises during our lovemaking, and I yearn to tease those sounds from her once more. It takes all my willpower not to reach out and trace the trails of light playing over her skin.

Purple and red lights explode against the view screen, coating us in a garish glow as the music dips into a low, mumbling groan. The ship jolts once. Twice. Then the deck starts to shudder.

The mood in the cabin shifts from wonder to nervousness bordering on panic. The once-lovely melody crescendos into a shrieking whine. *Something's wrong.* On instinct, I throw an arm over Suzanne just before wind blasts through the cabin and the air is spiked with the scent of ozone.

7

SUZANNE

My heart feels like it's going to explode from my chest. One minute I'm enjoying the amazing light display, and the next Kiozhi throws an arm over me and we're completely encased in foam. I can't see a thing. I can't even twitch a finger. At least I can breathe, despite what feels like foam up my nose, but my stomach is doing flip-flops because it feels like we're falling.

Holy fuck, are we about to crash?

My entire life flashes before my eyes. My parents, my sisters, my children… Why didn't I make one last call to my kids when I had a chance last night? I want to cry, but I'm too afraid.

Then we jar to a sudden stop. Like a vacuum seal releasing, the foam pressing around us lets go. I suck in a reflexive breath, eyes wide in the surrounding pitch darkness. At least the comforting pressure of Kiozhi's arm still wraps around my torso like an extra layer of protection. I really hope this is part of the show, but I know in my gut it probably isn't.

I squirm, pressing my arms against a flexible shell about an inch or so away from my body. I've never been claustrophobic, but I could easily develop a case of it right about now. Sliding one hand down to grip Kiozhi's arm, I speak into the darkness. "What's happening?"

The chiseled muscles of Kiozhi's arm flex, his deep voice sounding deliberately calm. "The safety foam only expands in the event of a crash."

My rapidly pounding heart squeezes in fear. *We crashed on an alien planet.* "Is the air out there breathable? Where are my sisters? Are they all right?" I realize I'm babbling, my voice getting shriller with every word, but I can't stop. My hands bat uselessly against the surrounding cocoon. "I need to get out of this seat. How do we get out?"

"I'm not sure." Kiozhi pulls his arm from my waist. "The safety pod should open when the foam dissolves. It seems to be malfunctioning."

I sense him pushing at the shell around us and join him, thinking this must be how baby sea turtles feel when they hatch. And just like those little turtles, we have no idea what sort of danger awaits us outside this shell.

Something cool sloshes around my ankles. Is it the dissolved foam? It feels like it's rising. "Is there supposed to be liquid in here?"

"No," Kiozhi grunts, straining harder. "There must be a crack in the emergency hull. I think we landed in water."

Dread fills my stomach. I push more frantically, trying to dig my nails into the material keeping us trapped as water rises up my shins. I realize I'm repeating, "Oh, God." My breath hitches. "I never called my kids. I don't want to die. Please don't let me die."

"Stay calm." Kiozhi's hands touch my face, turning me to face him, though I still can't see a thing in the darkness. "We must've landed in water, but I promise I will get you out of here."

I suck in a shuddering breath and nod fiercely as he withdraws his arm. I know I need to get myself under control, but I've never actually faced my own death before.

"What are you going to do?" I slide my hand across the seat, seeking his touch, but he's not there. Instead, something soft and spongy ripples beneath my fingertips. I recoil. *What the hell is that?*

Water climbs up the backs of my thighs and ass. It smells rank and swampy, like the time my kids came back from summer camp with wet swimming suits in their suitcases. My seat rocks violently, and I grip the arms of my chair. "Kiozhi!"

No answer. I slide my hand over to find my purse, which is wedged in the seat next to me, frantic to find anything that might help me escape. For almost two decades, I had a classic mom-purse full of everything under the sun. Of course for this trip I scaled down, and all I'm carrying now is a tiny cross-strap purse barely big enough for my phone, a tube of lipstick, and my sunglasses.

The water reaches my armpits, and I choke back a sob. *I'm going to die.*

Suddenly, the shell splits open and water rushes in. What feels like serrated teeth clamp onto my arm, and I'm dragged from my seat. Water goes up my nose and stings my eyes. I break the surface abruptly, and whatever was holding my arm releases me. I go flying through the air and hit the water again flat on my back, driving the air from my lungs.

Flailing, I try to rise to the surface. I reach it, choking and sputtering and blinking. Violent splashing draws my attention as I tread water, and I spin to see what looks like a gargantuan centipede with writhing legs. And it's coming straight for me.

With a choked yelp, I turn and paddle in the opposite direction. I can see what I think is the shore, but it feels a million miles away. Glow-in-the-dark plants line the bank, and massive trees climb toward the dark sky overhead. It's hard to breathe, and my arm stings. *This can't be happening.*

Something circles my foot, pulling me under. Water stings my sinuses. I can't see anything in the murky depths. I kick out with my other foot, dislodging whatever has hold of me. Bobbing to the surface, I swim for all I'm worth toward shore. My lungs ache and my heart knocks painfully against my ribs. Finally, I drag myself up the slippery bank, using handfuls of glowing foliage to pull myself free of the treacherous water.

Turning, I see the centipede monster rise from the surface. My jaw drops. Kiozhi is straddling it like an enormous mount.

"Run, Suzanne!" he shouts.

I turn, ready to flee, but then hesitate. I can't just leave him to fight this thing alone. Spotting a long, splintered branch, I grab it and hold it in front of me like a spear. No way I'm going back in the water, but if it comes my way, I'm going to do what I can to help.

The creature writhes and twists, mandibles clacking as it tries to dislodge its rider. Kiozhi's teeth are bared, and he rips one of the creature's antennas right off its head. The thing screeches and drops back into the water, taking Kiozhi with it. The surface ripples and bubbles.

One breath.

Two.

My heart jackhammers in my chest.

Still no sign of Kiozhi.

My arms start to tremble. This isn't possible. He can't have drowned. I hold my breath, waiting for him to emerge. A black tentacle whips up from the depths, smashing the near bank with a deafening crack. Water rises in a wave, cresting the bank and washing my feet out from under me. I land hard on my side, slipping in mud and leaves. Rolling to my knees, I see Kiozhi rising from the water. He's holding the creature's severed head by one antenna.

Tossing it aside, he steps onto the bank and kneels next to me, reaching for my arm. "You're hurt."

"Me? What about you?" I gape at him, surprised that he seems unscratched. Then I glance down at my arm.

A jagged gash circles my biceps where the thing must've grabbed me. Blood runs down my elbow and drips from my fingertips. Suddenly, my arm throbs and my fingertips feel numb. *Oh, God.* I've never been good with blood. My vision narrows, tightening to a pinprick. I glance back up to see Kiozhi's concerned eyes looking into mine. Then the world goes black.

51

8

KIOZHI

 catch Suzanne before she hits the ground, lowering her limp body gently to the mossy bank. My hands are covered in alien goo: a slippery purplish ooze that's more like mucus than blood. I don't want to foul her with it, but washing in the pond won't get me much cleaner, especially with the carcass now floating in the middle.

I'm still shaken from the attack. The creature hit me as I was resuming my human shape, and I barely hardened my matrix in time to defend myself. Then there was Suzanne, trapped in the pod while I fought. If the beast hadn't cracked the malfunctioning pod open with its thrashing, she might be dead now.

I scrub my hands clean on some nearby leaves and lean over to examine her unconscious form. She's pale, but her breathing sounds fine. The laceration on her arm from where the creature grabbed her doesn't appear to be deep, though she is still bleeding.

I sit back on my heels and survey our surroundings. We need a place to rest and see to our injuries. I know next to nothing about the Singing Planet, but it appears we've landed in a forest. Massive trees rise into darkness overhead, and multi-colored plants surround us, their leaves emitting a nebulous glow. Tree roots run like interlacing highways between the shrubbery, making line-of-sight impossible. I hope the other pods have landed nearby.

Standing, I call into the forest. "Hello? Can anyone hear me?"

Other than the soft creak of branches rubbing together, the forest is silent. My gut churns with worry. Our pod may not be the only one that malfunctioned. I bring up my ICC, but there isn't any signal. *Kuzara.* I guess it makes sense, since the planet isn't on the galactic grid, but it will make finding the other survivors extremely difficult.

I gather handfuls of large fallen leaves and scrub the slime from my body as best I can. Then I do the same for the cut on Suzanne's arm, removing the scarf she wears around her neck so I can use it as a bandage.

Once that's done, I glance at the floating carcass. Are there more of them in the area? I feel like we need to get away from here as soon as possible. I slide my arms under Suzanne's shoulders and knees to pick her up and carry her, but she rouses.

"What happened?" She sits up and looks around, her eyes widening when they settle on the pond. "Oh, God, it wasn't a dream."

"Unfortunately not." I gently touch the scarf on her arm. "How are you feeling?"

"It hurts, but I think I'm okay." She looks at me, stiffens, and turns her attention away. "Um, why are you naked?"

"Oh." With everything else going on, I hadn't considered it. I immediately have my matrix form a modesty shield over my genitals. "I had to use my amorphous form to escape the pod. My clothes are still inside."

Her eyes flick toward me, and my *Iki'i* senses her embarrassment shift to curiosity. "I forgot Kirenai could do that. Become… liquid."

Relieved I don't feel any revulsion coming from her, I chuckle. "Not liquid, exactly, but our natural state is semi-fluid. We don't use it very often because it's when we're most vulnerable. Other than that, Kirenai are impervious to most damage."

That seems to satisfy her, and she stands to look around. "Where's the shuttle?"

"I don't know. The escape pods must've jettisoned before it crashed."

She gulps and wraps her arms across her chest, shivering as if she's cold, though the air is almost stiflingly warm. "So everyone is scattered?" Her arms drop and she stands slightly taller, as if hit by an inspiration. "Hold on, my sister put an app on my phone. I might be able to use it to find her."

She opens the tiny bag hanging against her hip and the hope on her face collapses almost immediately. Tilting the small bag, she pours a stream of water from it, then pulls out a flat rectangle the size of her palm. "Dammit, it's soaked. It won't turn on." She shoves it back into her bag and spins in a slow circle. "Which way do we go?"

I look around and shrug. "Moving away from this pond is a good start."

We elbow our way through the bushes until we reach one of the massive roots humping up from the forest floor. She's about to pull herself on top of it when she cocks her head. "Do you hear that?"

I hold my breath and listen. There is a strange repetitive call echoing faintly between the trees. I think

I've heard it before, but I can't place it. "Yes. Do you recognize it?"

"I think that's Beanie!" She hauls herself up onto the massive root. "Beanie! Here, boy!"

I climb up and follow her, using the wide curved top of the root as a trail. "What's a Beanie?"

"My sister's dog." She bends over to crawl across a massive root, and I can't help but admire her ass. She's wearing loose pants made of a flowing green material that is slit up the front nearly to the tops of her thighs. Far too elegant for our current environment, but sexy enough to make my shaft stir. I tamp down my lust. This is the wrong time and place to pursue my courtship.

I follow her along the root, which creates a path between the glowing brush. It curves gently, meandering over the ground. The gullies and swells between it and the other roots create a maze with glowing plants sprouting in every nook and cranny. We're forced to climb several more roots as we follow the sound of the barking, calling out for survivors at regular intervals.

We're both panting and tired when the root we're following makes a sharp turn to skirt the bank of another pond. Thick shrubs grow along the edges, jutting from the water and obscuring the transition between land and shore.

Suzanne sucks in a sharp breath and takes a step backward, bumping into me. I instinctively put an arm around her to keep her from tripping. She presses her back against me, and I can't help the satisfied feeling I get from having her this close, regardless of the circumstances.

She whispers, "Do you think there's another one of those monsters in there?"

Narrowing my eyes, I look over the glistening surface and expand my *Iki'i*. A large predator is bound to give off at least some primitive emotions. "I don't sense anything."

We stand in silence for a few more moments studying the surface before she whispers, "Beanie stopped barking."

"What does that mean?" I ask.

"Either Tamara calmed him down or…" She shakes her head as a small shudder rolls through her.

I know what she's thinking. Her fear is valid, but there is nothing for us to do except press on. "Let's try to go around."

She nods. We backtrack to another cross-root, then follow a trail perpendicular to our previous direction. The path ends back at the pond.

"Shit." Suzanne loops an arm around my biceps and hugs it against her chest. "I'm so turned around. Is this the same pond or a different one?"

I shake my head, as uncertain as she is. Then I spot ripples fluttering across the surface of the pond. Something is moving in the water.

SUZANNE

I clutch Kiozhi's arm, too terrified breathe. There is something moving in the water. Then, beneath a cluster of purple leaves dangling over the water on the opposite bank, I see a familiar fawn-colored muzzle and two dark eyes.

"Beanie!" I let go of Kiozhi's arm and step forward. The tiny dog is trying to climb the opposite bank. When he hears my voice, he turns and paddles toward us, whining softly. That explains why he stopped barking. He must've fallen in and can't get out.

I'm fearful something will rise from below and devour him, but he reaches our side without incident, scrambling to find a way up.

Dropping to my knees, I reach down for him, but my arms aren't long enough.

"Let me," says Kiozhi, laying down on his belly.

The dog is also out of his reach, but not for long. His arm stretches, becoming disproportionately long until he grabs Beanie and pulls him free of the water. He sets the dog down and Beanie shakes, sending a spray of droplets over our laps. Then his tail starts wagging furiously. He puts his front paws on Kiozhi then wriggles over to me, tiny pink tongue darting out to kiss my chin when I bend down to pick him up.

"Good boy. Where's your momma?" I stand and look across the pond. "Tamara! Jennifer! Hello?"

There's no answer, which makes my heart ache with dread. I give Kiozhi an anguished look. "Tamara is never without her dog."

His lips thin as he nods. "We'll keep looking."

I cradle Beanie in one arm as we continue our search for a way around the pond. I'm trying not to dwell on what finding him alone might mean, but worry for my sisters makes my insides tremble.

Eventually, we reach the opposite side of the pond, thankfully without incident, but there's no sign of my sisters or any of the other pods. We keep walking. There doesn't seem to be a division between night and day on this planet, but it feels as if we've been walking for hours by the time we come upon a cave-like hollow in one of the massive trunks. The interior is dotted with bits of glowing golden moss.

Kiozhi gently takes Beanie from my arms. "This looks like a good place to rest."

I hadn't realized how heavy the dog had become until I was relieved of his weight. I don't want to stop searching, but I'm beyond tired. I nod reluctantly. "Yes."

The cave isn't large—barely big enough for us to lie down—but it's better than being in the open. The floor is covered with a spongy layer of dry leaves, and I sink down onto them gratefully. My stomach rumbles, and I realize my mouth is parched, but I'm too tired to deal with either of those things. I lay down on my side, shivering slightly. Kiozhi places Beanie against my stomach, and the little dog walks a tight circle before settling against me with a wuffly sigh. I pet his soft fur and close my eyes against tears of frustration.

Kiozhi's warmth settles against my back, and when he wraps one arm tightly around me to spoon against me, I don't even complain. As much as I tried to dodge his attention on the *Romantasy*, I'm really glad he's here with me now. I'm not sure how well I'd handle being stranded alone on this alien planet. His other hand slides up to stroke my hair, and I doze off.

I wake some time later with Kiozhi's arm still around me like a weighted blanket. Beanie has deserted me to tunnel under the leaves nearby, only his nose poking out. After a few minutes of reorienting myself to our situation, I wriggle onto my back and look over at his sleeping face. The golden glow of moss bathes his features, highlighting the classic lines and angles. His lashes are thick, dark crescents against his cheeks, and his slight dimples make me want to see him smile. He looks too perfect to be real.

His eyes open slowly, and he blinks at me. "Hey," he whispers.

Realizing I just got caught staring, I'm not sure what to say, so I just whisper back, "Hey."

He smiles and brushes his thumb over my cheekbone before plucking something from my hair. "You have leaves in your hair."

I reach up self-consciously and smooth my palm over my tangled tresses. My ex used to gaslight me all the time about my looks, trying to undermine my confidence. I never realized it until my therapist pointed it out after our divorce. But Kiozhi just smiles as if he thinks I'm cute, not passive-aggressively telling me I'm a rumpled mess. I'm struck by the sudden urge to kiss him.

Before I can stop myself, I *am* kissing him. Deeply. Hungrily.

He pulls me closer as my tongue meets his. His hand slides over my thigh to cup my ass, squeezing gently as he rocks his hips against me. The solid length of his erection presses against my belly, and a jolt of desire races through my blood. I know what he can do, and I want to feel that pleasure again. To leave my stress behind, even just for a moment. I moan into his mouth, and he responds by sliding one hand between my legs and rubbing gently over my crotch. *God, he's good at this.*

I reach down to stroke his hardness, discovering the covering over his crotch is gone, exposing his shaft to my touch. It's solid and hot, throbbing against my touch.

He presses my clit through the thin fabric of my pants, and I gasp. My panties are already drenched, my core pulsing with a need for more. I want him inside me *right now*. Breaking our kiss, I untie my waistband and shove my pants down my hips. He helps pull them free of my legs before lifting my tank top over my head. He cups my breasts in his palms, thumbs circling my nipples until sparks of lust race through me.

I widen my legs, drawing him between my knees. With one hand between us, I guide his erection to my opening. I gasp as he fills me in a swift, sure stroke. He feels so perfect inside me. My inner muscles contract almost immediately in climax. Even as I spasm, he pushes me higher with his strokes, his rhythm building into something primitive and wild that makes my blood sing.

He moans and thrusts, his eyes never leaving mine. I can't deny the connection I feel to him. I'm on the cusp of another release, riding it, surfing like a wave that refuses to crest.

Just when I think it will never break, he does a little circle with his hips, and I'm thrown over the edge, clenching around his huge cock. This time, Kiozhi isn't far behind. He explodes with a shudder, heat filling me and sending an aftershock of pleasure through my body.

He holds himself tight against my hips, pulsing with heat as he looks down into my face. I swear I see love filling his eyes. *Impossible.* He can't love me. We barely know each other. We're simply feeling connected in this impossible situation and needing to de-stress.

He rolls over and pulls me to lie on his chest, warm skin against warm skin. Beanie huffs and pokes his head from under a nest of leaves, then burrows back out of sight. I blink and sigh deeply, sleep threatening to drag me under once more.

I know we should get up and continue our search, but I don't want to move, not quite yet. I gaze toward the back of our shelter, looking over the glowing moss and other small plants. Growing things have always been one of my passions, and these would make a spectacular moon garden back on Earth.

Back on Earth. Out of nowhere, a sob overtakes me. Will I ever see home again? My kids?

Kiozhi's arm tightens around me, and he kisses the top of my head, a gesture so sweet it makes me sob again. I don't like feeling this vulnerable and needy, especially with a guy who basically stalked me not too long ago. I push up to a sitting position and search for my clothes. "Stop being so nice to me," I grit through my teeth, feeling stupid as tears threaten to spill from my eyes. "This doesn't mean we're a couple. It was just a moment of weakness."

"Suzanne—"

I know I'm being a bitch, but if I look at him, I'll break down, and that's the last thing we need. "Come on." I stand and pull on my pants, moving out of the cave before I even have them tied in place. "We need to find the others."

10

KIOZHI

Stunned by Suzanne's outward reaction to my affection, I lay on the leaves for a moment after she departs. My *Iki'i* insists she enjoys my tenderness, but her words and body language indicate otherwise. Which truth am I to believe?

Rising, I stretch until my fingertips brush the cave ceiling. I feel better after resting, but my stomach feels like it's gnawing a hole through me.

The carpet of leaves rustles, and I remember the dog. Suzanne must be too agitated to remember he's with us, and those tiny legs won't be able to keep up well, especially if we have to do more climbing. I bend down and push aside the leaves. "Are you ready to travel, little man?"

Beanie shakes off the rest of the leaves and stretches, small mouth opening in a wide pink yawn. His hind quarters wiggle furiously, and he prances in front of me, front paws batting the air with excitement.

I smile indulgently and pick him up. He's soft and warm, settling into the crook of my arm as I catch up to Suzanne.

She's studying an enormous branch laying across the root she's following. "It looks like this was recently broken, possibly from the shuttle."

I examine the purple bark and scattered leaves. The area looks exactly the same as everything else we've encountered. "How can you tell it's recent?"

"The sap is fresh. Smell it?" There is a slightly vegetal scent in the air nearby. She points at the splintered end of the branch with glistening beads of pinkish fluid. Then she points toward the canopy. "And there's a gash in that trunk that may be from a recent impact. See? It looks like it's bleeding sap."

I look up and nod. "That's good reasoning. I never would've noticed these details. Are you a plant specialist?"

A flush rises to her cheeks, and I sense a flicker of pride. "I took a few horticulture classes while the kids were in school, but I couldn't carry a full course load, take care of the house, and work a full-time job. Though I suppose I did manage to keep us fed and clothed, so I guess it was worth the sacrifice. Besides, I never was a straight-A student." She sighs and picks up the end of a thick vine tangled around the limb. "That's why I supported my ex while he got his M.D. Instead of the other way around."

Waves of self-loathing pulse from her, strong enough to make me nauseous, and my own thoughts are now in turmoil. She has offspring? I thought the IDA had specifically picked women who hadn't yet experienced mates and children. Not that it matters to me in the end. "Is this male you refer to as your ex the one who sired your children?"

She laughs, a pitiless sound. "That is an excellent description of him."

I don't like the change in her emotions when she talks about this male. "You supported him… but never the other way around?"

"If there's one thing I learned while I was married, it's that relationships are never balanced evenly." She turns and steps over the fallen branch, continuing along the root snaking between the tall brush. "Robbie wrung me dry and tossed me aside. I will never allow that to happen to me again." The venom in her voice is painful to hear. Even Beanie whines from where he rests in the crook of my arm.

"I would never treat you that way," I say softly.

Suzanne does an about-face and glares. "No, you won't, because we're not in a relationship. I just told you I will never allow that to happen again."

Everything I know about her now clicks into place. I understand why she's been avoiding me. Much of her life has been spent in service to a man who didn't deserve her. I'm certain I've found my second-chance mate, but she may be too wounded to recognize me as hers. I sigh and bow my head. "I see."

"Good." Pivoting, she continues walking.

I follow slightly behind, full of questions but concerned they might make her angry. Finally, I decide to ask about plants again. "Do you ever intend to resume your studies?"

She glances over her shoulder toward me, eyebrows raised. "I told you my grades suck."

"Your grades don't matter, as long as you're learning something you love."

Her steps slow, allowing me to draw up beside her. "Actually, I start classes at the community college when I get home."

I smile. "Excellent. Perhaps you can take samples home with you from here."

"That would be fun, though I wouldn't want to introduce an invasive species."

We continue to talk about horticulture on her planet as we follow the path of broken foliage. Beanie scouts ahead of us, running back to check on us now and again. Eventually, we reach a mass of splintered roots and branches laying haphazardly over a deeply carved trench in the forest floor. A ragged piece of the shuttle's purple hull lays half buried in the dirt.

"Look." I point toward a vacant escape pod poking up from the brush. "There's another pod." Beanie is already sniffing around the trench.

"Hello!" Suzanne calls.

Nobody answers our shouts. We follow the gouged landscape until we reach the nose of the shuttle butted up against a tree. Another empty escape pod rests nearby—a single that can only be from inside the cockpit.

I poke my head inside what remains of the shuttle's cockpit. "Tazhio? Anybody here?"

There's no sign of my friend, just damaged control panels and crumpled hull plating. Worry coils inside me, but there are no bodies, so I take it as a good sign.

"Tamara was with the pilot." Suzanne stands next to me and looks inside. "Do you think they're okay?"

"I don't know, but Tazhio will do everything in his power to keep your sister safe."

"Assuming their pods didn't malfunction too."

I swallow thickly and nod. "That was unusual. Let's hope they just went in search of the other passengers."

Her brow is furrowed, and I want to offer better comfort, but after what happened in the cave, I'm not sure I should. Usually, my *Iki'i* gives me an edge in my personal interactions, but Suzanne's inner conflict poses an uncertainty I'm at a loss to resolve.

She takes a step inside the destroyed cockpit. "Any chance we might find food or water in here? I'm starving."

My stomach has also been complaining. I glance around hopefully, but recalling the way the cockpit looked before we left the *Romantasy*, I think it's safe to assume there isn't. "I doubt it." Taking her arm, I gently pull her back out of the cockpit. "I think we're going to have to find something local."

We climb the other side of the trench, loose dirt and branches giving way under our hands and feet. When we reach the top, Suzanne points to a spot farther along the edge. "That area looks like it's been trampled."

We navigate over and around debris to reach it. Broken branches and fallen leaves cover the ground, and the edge looks sloughed, as if someone had difficulty climbing it. Small yellow orbs covered in spikes litter the ground. Suzanne picks one up. "This looks like a large grain of pollen. Ouch!" She drops the orb as if it burns, rubbing her fingers against the front of her pants. "Shit, don't touch those. Might be poisonous. My fingers are tingling."

I frown, looking up at the branches high above us. "They may be falling off the trees. Let's move."

She nods, and we slide back down to where Beanie has been sniffing along the wall of the trench. Suzanne picks him up, but as we walk away, he squirms free and takes off barking. In the blink of an eye, he's up the trench wall and disappearing into the brush.

"Beanie, come!" Suzanne yells, climbing up after him. "Beanie!"

I hurry to follow but pause at a churned spot of dirt. There are indentations that look like paws. Not small ones like Beanie's—human-sized. With claws. I frown. Could it be a Kirenai? I try to think of any beings that might leave these tracks, but I know of none that have six toes.

I glance up at where Suzanne and Beanie have already disappeared in the brush.

"*Kuzara,*" I say, vaulting up the side of the trench. Suzanne is heading straight toward whatever made these prints.

"*Kuzara,*" I say, vaulting up the side of the trench. Suzanne is heading straight toward whatever made these prints.

11

SUZANNE

Beanie moves quickly through the brush ahead, dodging beneath the understory with ease. My slit-leg pants are definitely not made for bushwhacking, catching on everything as I crash through the dense brush after him, and my exposed skin stings with scratches. I push past a glowing fuchsia plant with multi-lobed leaves and nearly trip over what looks like an azure sea fan. This planet reminds me of a coral reef, only without the water or any lively fish darting among the plants. In fact, other than the enormous creature that attacked us at the pond, we've encountered no animal life at all, which seems strange.

But that isn't my concern right now. I can't afford to lose track of Beanie. He must've picked up Tamara's scent. Behind me, I hear Kiozhi rustling and cursing. "Suzanne, wait. We don't know—"

"I think he smells something," I shout back.

Beanie has climbed up onto another root path and is circling with his nose to the ground. I don't know how he got up there so quickly, because I need a minute to pull myself up behind him. I hope my sister stayed on the trail from here on.

Kiozhi joins us, grabbing my arm. "We need to slow down. I saw clawed footprints back there."

I hadn't even considered that Beanie might be chasing something besides Tamara. "Well, crap." I pat my thighs with both hands. "Beanie, come here!"

The dog darts away as I approach, gleefully ignoring me.

"Come back here, you little rat-chaser!" I take off after him.

Kiozhi pulls me up short. "Stop. Whatever he's chasing is at least as big as we are, and there may be more than one."

My chest tightens. "My sister will be devastated if anything happens to her dog." I pat my thighs again. "Beanie, want a cookie?"

I think he knows I'm lying about the cookie because he gives me a disdainful look before trotting down the trail with a jaunty twitch of his rump.

"Dammit, Beanie!"

Kiozhi moves ahead. "Let me go first. If we encounter danger, run."

I pause to pick up a hefty branch I can use as a club. For better or for worse, Kiozhi and I are in this together, and I don't plan to abandon him now, no matter what he says.

We chase the dog for a while without incident. I'm starting to think Kiozhi's fears are unfounded when suddenly Beanie yelps.

Ahead of me, Kiozhi comes to a sudden stop, and I lean sideways to see around him. A ten-foot-tall bush with enormous, fleshy, arrowhead-shaped maroon leaves and thin, curling tendrils covered in what look like dangling yellow berries looms over the trail about thirty feet away. Beanie stands facing the plant, baring his teeth and growling.

I grip my club and raise it like a baseball bat, expecting some sort of monster to burst from the shrubbery.

Instead, the plant's tendrils lash out. Beanie yelps again, dancing out of the way while continuing his barking.

"Oh, shit!" I try to push past Kiozhi, but he's already moving forward.

The tendrils whip toward the dog again, and this time one of them loops around Beanie's middle. He struggles, but the vine lifts him into the air. One of the fleshy maroon leaves splits open like a six-petaled flower. Except it's not like a flower at all, but more like a mouth, dripping saliva and making sucking sounds. The tendril swings the wriggling dog closer, trying to position him over the flower.

"Beanie!" I scream.

Kiozhi reaches Beanie and grabs him by his hind legs. With a swift jerk, he snaps the tendril, freeing the dog. He steps backward, but before he can move out of range, a vine shoots out and captures his ankle. His feet are yanked out from under him. He crashes backward onto the trail. Beanie's small form tumbles from his grip and rolls off into the brush.

I halt about ten feet away from Kiozhi. My heart thunders against my ribs. How the hell do you fight a carnivorous plant? I need a torch or a machete, not a useless stick.

Another flower opens, much bigger than the one that tried to eat Beanie. The tendril around Kiozhi's ankle jerks him along the ground, ever closer to the pulsing flower mouth as he struggles to unwrap himself. Now that I can see inside the flower's maw, I notice what look like hundreds of tiny teeth, each dripping what I suspect are digestive juices.

It's an alien version of a Venus Flytrap—a huge, man-eating version.

Kiozhi frees his ankle, but more tendrils have wrapped around his wrist and other ankle. For every one he breaks, two more ensnare him.

I move closer and extend my club, praying I'm not in range of the plant's lashing vines. "Grab the stick. I'll help pull you free."

"You need to run," he says, ignoring me as he tears through another vine.

"Come on, before it drags you any closer."

With a frustrated grunt, Kiozhi breaks his wrist free and rolls over onto his belly, taking the end of my club in one hand. His bound legs are useless, but his free hand claws the path, dragging himself forward as I lean back to add my weight to the pull. He now has at least five tendrils around his legs, and the plant has bent over toward him, flower mouth wrapping around his foot. It makes disgusting slurping sounds, and I have the horrible mental image of it stripping the flesh off Kiozhi's bones.

"Hold on!" I grunt, putting every fiber of my being into holding onto the club. The rough bark stings my palms, but I refuse to let go. I feel like I'm playing tug-of-war: heaving, heaving, heaving.

Kiozhi's teeth are bared with effort. We seem to be evenly matched with the plant. In a moment of terror, I realize the plant is slowly climbing up the trail after us.

"Kiozhi!" My eyes are wide on the monster.

Glancing back at the creature, Kiozhi returns his attention to me. "Save yourself," he says through clenched teeth. "Run."

I know what he's about to do, and I can't bear it. Not just because I don't want to be alone, but because Kiozhi doesn't deserve this. He's a good man. I grit my teeth. "No. Fucking. Way."

Beanie pops out of the bushes, growling. He clamps his teeth around a tendril and tugs. The tendril shudders and releases its grip on Kiozhi. More tendrils whip toward the dog, but Beanie lets go in the nick of time, dashing away.

It's enough of a distraction for Kiozhi to jerk one leg free of the free of its remaining tendril. He pulls his knee under him and strains forward, still gripping the club with one hand. "*Kuzara*," he groans. "Keep pulling. I have an idea."

His trapped leg flexes and thins, seeming to flow upward toward his body. The flower mouth clamped around his foot snaps shut, pulsing in a strange, gulping motion. Kiozhi grunts in pain and lurches forward.

Without his foot.

"Oh, God!" I yelp, helping him crawl several yards away. "What the hell just happened?"

"I sacrificed part of my matrix."

"Jesus," I breathe, understanding why the plant looked like it was swallowing. "Did that plant *eat* a part of you?"

"Yes."

I stop and let him sag to the ground, both of us panting. His foot and leg have reformed, but his shin and calf look raw, seeping a blue-tinged liquid. "How bad are you?" I ask. My concern is like a boulder inside my chest. "I thought you said Kirenai are impervious to most damage."

He's breathing in heaving gulps, and his face looks ashen beneath his blue skin. "Yes, unless we're in our amorphous state. Then I'm pretty helpless."

I grab one of my pant legs and tear a strip free so I can bind his injured leg. I'm not even sure that will help, but I have to do something.

Beanie emerges from the bushes and joins us. He's panting, and a large patch of fur is missing from one hip. The skin looks raw but not bloody. Kiozhi reaches out and strokes his head. "Thank you, little man. You saved my life."

I glance behind us toward the plant and gasp. It's slowly shambling onto the trail after us.

"Shit. That plant's still after us. We need to get away from here." I put a shoulder under Kiozhi's arm and help him stand.

He wobbles and sags against me.

Supporting as much of his weight as I can, I help him limp in the direction we came from, trying not to trip over Beanie, who's apparently decided it's better to stay close to us. We have to stop and rest several times, but at least we seem to have left the plant behind. I really hope it can't track us.

During one rest break, I notice a dark spot at the base of a trunk just off the trail. I squint through the dim light cast by the glowing plants. "Is that a cave?"

Kiozhi seems to be having trouble keeping his eyes open. "We should go see."

My heart races as we step off the trail. So far, this planet has given us nothing but danger, and I'm not sure how much more we can take.

12

SUZANNE

I stumble under Kiozhi's weight. He leans on me more and more as we struggle through the brush toward the cave until I'm almost dragging him along. I examine the foliage ahead as we move. The light from the pastel-colored foliage is murky at best, making me feel like I'm in a sci-fi horror movie.

We reach the tree, but my heart falls at the sight of the darkened bark. "Shit, this isn't a cave. Just a discolored part of the trunk."

Kiozhi lets out a grunt I think is disappointment and sags to the forest floor. His body feels hotter than I remember, and he closes his eyes with a sigh as Beanie climbs tiredly onto his lap.

I stand up straight to stretch my aching back. I should be sweating up a storm after our walk, but my skin is papery and dry. My mouth feels like cotton, and my stomach is so empty I feel like I'm about to turn inside out. We need to find water, but Kiozhi's in no condition to search with me.

"Stay here and rest. I'm going to find water," I say, looking around. After our initial encounter, the thought of approaching a pond by myself is terrifying, but I don't see any other choice.

"Wait." Kiozhi points to the right. "You hear that?"

It sounds like something dripping. I follow the sound and find a bank of turquoise vines hiding what looks like a three-foot-high hole beneath one of the massive roots. Nervously, I push the vines aside to reveal an underground cavern. The same golden moss I noticed in the other cave covers the walls, giving the space the same gentle light as the surrounding forest. Intertwining roots and vines form a lattice I think we can climb to get in and out.

Better yet, there's a thin trickle of water running down the wall on the far side. It forms a tiny pool before streaming away under the spongy gray leaves covering the floor. "It's a cave!" I call back to Kiozhi. "And there's water too. I'm going to check it out."

"Not without me," Kiozhi says as I swing my feet over the lip. He tries to sit up but ends up sagging onto his elbow. His face is pinched with agony, and he shakes his head. "Maybe not. But at least take a weapon."

He has a good point. I pick up a hefty branch, then swing my feet over the edge and drop inside.

The cave is about twelve or fifteen feet in diameter and seven or eight feet high. It slopes downward toward the back where the stream runs along the wall. There are a few spots of round fuchsia leaves growing in the corners near the ceiling, but they don't seem to be moving. I don't see any other cracks or openings leading to other caves.

Stepping carefully across the floor in case the dead leaves hide pitfalls, I move toward the spring. The air here is sweet, like a ripe peach, full of life yet layered with the subtle scent of decay. I scoop a handful of water from the pool and smell it. There isn't any foul scent, so I take a tiny sip. The cool water coats my parched tongue, and I suddenly want to drop to my knees and lap up the water like a dog.

I take a bigger gulp. The water hits my empty stomach like a brick, and my gut heaves. I gasp, remembering all those spaghetti westerns Dad used to watch where people who've been wandering in the desert throw up after drinking too fast. Guess that part wasn't fiction.

Swallowing back the nausea, I go back to the entrance and call for Kiozhi to climb down. He hands Beanie to me, then I hover behind Kiozhi as he clumsily descends. The instant his feet hit the bottom, he drops to his knees and flops over so he's half propped against the wall. "I'm sorry."

"Don't apologize. You're hurt. Let me bring you some water." I head for the pool.

Beanie is already there, lapping greedily. It's only two feet in diameter, so I wait until he's done, then empty my purse and rinse it out before filling it—not the most sanitary container, but it works. I return and offer it to Kiozhi. "Not too much. We can't be certain it's safe."

"I don't care at this point," Kiozhi says between gulps. The water runs down his forearms and drips from his elbows, glistening as it hits his muscular chest. I don't understand how he can be so sexy at a time like this, but even injured, he's beautiful.

I return to the pool, glad to see the spring has already refreshed the water. Ignoring my own warning, I drink until my stomach aches with fullness, then scrub water over my face and arms, glad to feel cleaner. "I can't believe how lucky we are to have found this place."

Kiozhi sits with his back against the wall, Beanie once more curled on his lap. His fingers toy with the small dog's ear. The two seem to have developed a bond, which I have to admit is sort of cute.

"Come, sit." Kiozhi pats the leaves beside him. He still looks tired, but the water seems to already be making him feel better.

I shake my head. "I should go find food before I'm too tired to look."

"Let the water rejuvenate you first." He lifts an arm, inviting me to snuggle against him.

I know I said we aren't a couple, but the temptation to accept his comfort is too great. We've been through a lot together—I can forgive myself for wanting to be close. And it seems he's incapable of holding a grudge.

I settle next to him, resting my cheek on his pecs. My eyes immediately want to drift closed. The glowing moss on the wall behind us is plush and velvety, and the floor of leaves is as plush as my pillow-top mattress back home. I sigh. No more words pass between us, and I don't know how much time has passed before I open my eyes again. Kiozhi's breathing is steady under my cheek, his arm warm around my shoulders, but his skin no longer seems feverish. I smile with relief.

My stomach is a gnawing ache that won't let me sleep, so I ease myself out of his embrace. I thought I saw a plant with things that look like berries not too far from here, and it should only take me a couple of minutes to gather some.

Beanie opens one eye to look at me, then closes it again as if to say, "You're on your own."

I rub his head, then go take another long drink of water. My phone, sunglasses, and lipstick are still scattered next to the pool, so I shove them back into my purse before I scale the wall and exit the cave.

I can see the mint-green bushes with clustered raspberry-shaped fruits down in a hollow next to a decaying log. Despite how close they are, my pulse races as I move toward them, trying to keep my footsteps as quiet as possible. I feel like I need eyes in the back of my head. I brush my anxiety aside. Kiozhi is injured and needs food to recover—I'm the only one capable of finding it.

When I reach the bushes, I glance around to be certain nothing is stalking me before picking a berry. It's soft and very juicy. I squeeze it until glowing green juice coats my fingers. There don't appear to be any seeds, and it smells sweet and citrusy.

I chew the inside of my cheek. My girls earned a badge for wilderness survival, and I remember how to test the edibility of wild plants, but these are alien. They glow in the dark, for heaven's sake. Do the same rules apply?

My stomach grumbles loudly, prodding me to touch the tip of one juice-covered finger against my tongue. My eyelids twitch at the sour taste and my mouth puckers. I like lemon flavor, but this is downright acidic, like drinking raw vinegar. I swallow again and again to clear my palate, wishing I had some water. At least I haven't gone blind or keeled over on the spot. I smack my lips. No numbness or stomach cramps yet. Still, these are too sour to consider palatable, at least until I'm out of other options.

I toss the berry aside, wiping my fingers on some nearby leaves as I look around the edges of the hollow.

On top of a root near the trunk of a tree sprawls a mat of dull yellow foliage covered with golden brown nodules the size and shape of kiwi fruit. They look promising.

I glance over my shoulder again, making sure I can still see the cave. The trunks all look alike, and it would be easy to lose my way. The last thing I want to do is to get separated from Kiozhi. I shake my head at the irony. On the ship, I worked so hard to evade him—I was downright mean when he sat next to me on the shuttle. Yet if he hadn't joined me, I'd probably be dead right now, drowned in the pod or digesting inside the belly of the centipede monster. The longer I'm with him, the more I realize I've grown to like him. He's a good guy, not at all selfish like my ex. He even stepped in when the Venus Flytrap tried to eat Beanie, and what does the little dog offer in terms of survival?

I climb up onto the roots next to the yellow plant and open my cross-strap purse to retrieve my lipstick, using it to mark the nearby trunk with an arrow pointing toward the cave. The pale pink isn't startlingly visible, but I should be able to find it again if I look.

Bending down, I grasp one of the kiwi lookalikes and tug.

Like I just pulled a lever, the matted leaves sweep up and engulf my hand. I scream and pull free. My entire hand is covered in something sticky, and my skin burns.

I need to wash this stuff off *now*.

13

KIOZHI

Something startles me awake. A noise? I'm aching and disoriented. The air smells sweet and fruity, almost like regeneration fluid, but I'm not in my resting state. And I'm definitely not in my resting pod. A small wet tongue flicks against my face, and I open my eyes to a small quadruped hardly bigger than my head licking me. *Beanie.*

Everything comes back in a rush. I push myself to sitting, and the dog wriggles onto my lap, whining softly. His poor skin looks mottled and bruised where he lost fur during the attack, but he seems to be recovering. I scratch behind his ears. "Good boy."

I look around the small cave for Suzanne, but there's no sign of her. Where did she go? I frown at Beanie, who whines again. My stomach tightens with worry. *Perhaps she just stepped outside to relieve herself.*

"Suzanne!" I shout, voice loud in the cave.

No response.

I stand and test my weight on my injured limb. The water and rest have rejuvenated me considerably, though the fabric tied around my leg is stiff with blood. I haven't been wounded like this since I was a small child, before I learned to harden my form. My friends and I were trying our hand at carving, and I still remember my parents' distress when I stumbled home dripping blood.

Limping over to the opening, I peer outside. I can't see much beyond the veil of vines. "Suzanne? Are you out there?"

Still only silence.

My worry turns to dread. She should've woken me so I could at least be on standby. I might be weak, but I'd give my life to protect her, even if all I can be is a distraction so she can escape.

I grasp the lattice when a yip reminds me that Beanie can't get out by himself.

"All right, little man. Come on." I pick him up and put him outside.

Just then, Suzanne stumbles into view clutching one hand against her chest. I step back so she can get into the cave. She drops to the floor with a thud, not even bothering with the lattice. She's breathing hard, and my *Iki'i* thrums under her fear.

"What happened?" I ask. "Are you all right?"

She extends her right hand to show me raised red welts covering her delicate skin. "I found another carnivorous plant."

I grasp her undamaged arm, guiding her toward the pool. "You shouldn't have gone out alone."

"I just wanted to find food, and I didn't plan to go far."

"I can't lose you, Suzanne. Don't do that again. Please."

Sluicing water over her hand, I gently rub away some sort of slippery substance coating her skin. She flinches at first, then relaxes as I wash the back of her hand, her palm, between each finger to be certain I don't miss a spot. It's totally the wrong time and place, but touching her makes my balls ache.

"Kiozhi." Suzanne's voice is a little husky. "I think you got it."

I snap my gaze to hers, realizing I'm now washing up to the crook of her elbow, well beyond the welts covering her hand. Yet she doesn't pull away. Her lips are parted, her breathing quickened.

It would be so easy to bend down and kiss her. To take her again. *Kuzara*, I could claim her right now. But that would only create a shell of a relationship. I want her to embrace our bond, not resent it. So I pull back and reluctantly release her hand.

"Better?"

"Yes, thank you."

Beanie barks from outside, and she goes over to help him down. He snuffles her, then trots over and nudges my injured leg.

"I'm all right, little man." I pat his head. For such a small creature, he has a lot of empathy. "Thanks for checking."

"How's your leg?" Suzanne pulls aside one edge of my bandage. Dark spots on the fabric show where I've started bleeding again.

"The bandage helps." I'm feeling better, though not completely healed.

She makes a doubtful noise before gently unwinding it. "This looks terrible."

I lean over to look at the abraded skin. "As long as the blood is mostly clear, I'm okay."

"But there's dirt in the wound. Even you could be vulnerable to infection." Tearing off a fresh strip from her pant leg, she washes and re-bandages my leg, then sits back on her heels to review her work.

"Are you okay to walk again? We should try to find food."

"Yes, if we take it slow."

We exit the cave again, and she finds me a branch I can use as a crutch. Though I enjoy having an excuse to touch her, she needs to be able to run without worrying about me. Plus, it would be good to have a weapon in hand.

We move along the trail, and she points to a matted yellow plant. "That's the thing that tried to eat my hand."

I nod. "We need to approach every single thing here as dangerous."

"Yes," she agrees. "Though I'm getting hungry enough to bite back."

I chuckle, and we continue looking for plants that could be edible. Beanie scouts ahead, but not as far as he did earlier, and Suzanne's usually perky movements have grown more lethargic. Each step I take feels leaden. Without food, none of us will be able to carry on much longer.

Suzanne keeps track of our path by marking the trunks with a waxy pink color stick she stores in her purse. I may be driven to protect her, but without her, I'd probably end up wandering around in circles on this hostile planet—or worse.

We pause to rest along the trail. Suzanne sighs. "I wish we had a way to carry water."

"What about your purse?" I ask.

She shakes her head. "It leaks."

Suddenly, Beanie lets out a joyful yip and darts off into the bushes.

"Not again," groans Suzanne. "I swear that mutt has no regard for danger."

I suppress a smile, thinking of how she went off to find food by herself, but refrain from making the comparison out loud.

The dog returns and lowers himself on his front legs, yipping again as if expecting something.

I focus my *Iki'i*. There's a sense of joyful anticipation about him. "I think he wants us to follow."

Suzanne sighs. "Why not?"

We step down off the trail.

"His barking is going to attract more trouble if he doesn't stop," I say.

Then his barking does stop, and we hear a faint female voice calling, "Beanie, come!"

Suzanne grabs my arm. "That sounds like Tamara!"

14

SUZANNE

I pull Kiozhi's arm around my shoulder, helping him hurry through the tangled bushes. My heart beats faster with each step, and I smell what I hope is campfire smoke.

"Tamara!" I shout. "Tamara, it's me!" I don't think she can hear me over Beanie's yapping.

We round a tree, and I nearly run straight into Jennifer.

Kiozhi drops his arm as my sister throws her arms around me. "Oh my God, Suzanne! I knew you'd find us!"

Shocked and delighted, I clutch her back. Tears of joy flow down my cheeks, and when Tamara joins us seconds later, I grab her in a bear hug too. "I'm so glad you're both okay!"

Crying, all three of us simply hold each other.

When I regain control of my sniffling and break away, I see the shuttle pilot, Tazhio, helping Kiozhi to his feet. Tazhio wears a one-piece flight suit with the top half hanging around his hips, leaving his blue chest and arms bare. "How'd you get injured?" he asks Kiozhi.

"I'd like to say it was your terrible landing," Kiozhi says with a smirk. "But I'm embarrassed to admit I was nearly consumed by a hostile plant."

Jennifer tugs at my purse. "Where's your phone, Suzanne? I need it."

"Seriously, Jennifer?" I jerk my purse away and glower at her. "Is astronomy the only thing you think about? I almost died out there. More than once."

She scowls back. "We've all almost died. And this isn't about my thesis. I'm making a rescue beacon."

My indignation dissolves. If anyone can cobble together technology for a beacon, it's my brainy little sister. I sigh and retrieve my phone from my purse. "Here. But it got wet. It's dead."

She takes it and walks away, head bent over the dark screen. That girl has a one-track mind.

"We have food and water," says Tamara. "But before we go back to camp, we need to know if you encountered any monsters? Flying monsters, specifically?"

My heart skips a beat. I thought the gargantuan centipede and carnivorous plants were horrible enough. "Shit! Are there flying monsters on this planet too?"

"Yes. You haven't seen any?"

"No, nothing like that."

"Oh, thank God." Tamara loops her arm through mine. "Come on."

Tazhio helps support Kiozhi as we push through more bushes, emerging into a clearing next to a small pond. A cheery fire burns on the shore, and several more passengers rise to greet us—a red-haired Fogarian, a small, gray Hage in a crew uniform, and a Kirenai in a yellow Speedo.

Another Kirenai with a bald head and muscles like an ox sits propped against a nearby tree trunk—Nazhin, the porter who was with us on the shuttle. Jennifer's already sitting next to him, setting our phones in a line on the ground. He raises a hand and plays with a strand of her hair. She smiles back at him in a way I haven't seen her smile since, well, ever. I raise an eyebrow. *I knew there was a vibe between them back on the shuttle.*

On board the *Romantasy,* I thought the Kirenai looked like clones, and I'm surprised to realize how different the four here appear now. Tazhio with his large eyes, Nazhin with his bald head, the Ken doll Kirenai in a

Speedo, and Kiozhi, who's developed a more hardened GQ look since we crashed. His cheekbones are sharper, his nose more Roman. Even injured, he's sexier than any man I've met before. Or maybe it's *because* he's injured; it's hard to resist a self-sacrificing hero.

A booming voice near the fire startles me. "Greetings!" The Fogarian beams at me and fluffs a stack of leaves next to him. "My name is Erud, and I would be honored to have you sit beside me."

"Oh, that's um, thank you, but I'm good here." I sit next to Kiozhi—the devil you know, as the saying goes. I definitely don't need more aliens trying to gain my attention.

Erud's crimson mustache droops, but he doesn't say anything else.

"I'm called Ubi, and this is Hanzu." The Hage in the crew uniform gestures toward the Kirenai in the yellow Speedo. "Would the two of you care for some food?" He offers us something that looks like purple golf balls.

"God, yes, please," I say, reaching for one.

He shows us how to twist a ball in half, revealing a juicy center. The pulp tastes like ambrosia, and I'm thrilled when it turns out they have an entire basket to share.

Tamara sits with Beanie on her lap, feeding him something that looks like a long white French fry. She offers me one, too. It crunches like a carrot and tastes like cardboard, but it's somehow satisfying enough that I take a second one. Kiozhi devours several sticks and twists open golf balls in rapid succession, handing me an open half almost before I've finished the half I have.

I look around the rest of the sparse camp. "Are we the only survivors?"

"We haven't found everyone yet," says Tazhio somberly.

There's a strange tenseness in the air, as if nobody wants to say more. "What?" I ask.

Tamara takes a deep breath. "We did find one other human. A woman named Sophia. She…" She lets out a shaky breath. "She was infected."

"Infected?" I'm suddenly no longer hungry and lower my half-eaten cardboard stick to my lap. "With what?"

Tazhio scratches behind one ear. "There's a parasite on this planet the locals call a Gloor. It hunts fertile women to lay its eggs in them. When the eggs hatch, the spawn eat their way out of the host's body and attack anyone nearby. The locals, they call themselves Sheeghr, keep their females perpetually pregnant to stave off the parasite. They recognized that Sophia was infected and…" he tapers off to glance at Tamara.

I stare at him. Impregnated by an alien parasite? The more I learn about this planet, the more I feel like I've been dropped into a horror film. "What happened to her?"

He presses his lips into a tight line. "We couldn't keep her here with us. The Sheeghr took her."

I can't even breathe, let alone speak. Kiozhi says what I'm thinking. "To do what?"

Tamara's lip trembles, and tears fill her eyes before she looks away. "Put her out of her misery."

Tazhio puts an arm around Tamara as she cries softly, and his voice has a gravelly edge to it. "There wasn't anything we could do to help her, not without advanced medical technology. We couldn't risk keeping her with us, especially since we don't know when or if we'll ever be rescued."

Everyone else stares morosely at their hands. What they've told me is too horrible to even imagine. Then I realize. "Wait—when or if we're rescued? What do you mean? Surely people are looking for us?"

Tazhio takes a deep, pained breath. "Sensors and signals can't penetrate this planet's ionosphere. That's why a special license is required to fly—"

Tamara lifts her cheek from his chest and gives him a hard look. "Not your fault, Tazhio. And we mustn't give up hope. Jennifer thinks she can get a signal through."

The food I just ate churns below my ribs. Jennifer's brilliant, but if aliens who can build starships haven't already figured out how to make a rescue beacon work here, I doubt she's going to be able to create one using a bunch of smartphones. It sounds to me like we're stuck here permanently.

"I hate this fucking planet." I clutch my arms tightly around my ribs, thinking about giant centipedes, carnivorous plants, and now a flying parasite. "How are we going to keep ourselves alive?"

Tamara's worried eyes meet mine. "The Gloor is only attracted to fertile women. I'm already pregnant, and Jennifer's birth control protects her."

I frown. "You haven't had a boyfriend in years. How can you be pregnant?"

She laces her fingers with Tazhio's. "That's a story all by itself. The short version is that Tazhio and I are now mates."

I open my mouth to argue that they just met, that getting pregnant so quickly is impossible, then snap my jaw shut. I was only with Robbie a few weeks in high school before I got knocked up. It's totally possible. "But how could you possibly *know* you're pregnant? We've only been here a few days."

"The Sheeghr can sense it," she says.

I want to argue again, but I've never seen my sister glow like this, full of confidence and contentment. I want to be happy for her, yet icy dread is slowly creeping through my veins. My tubal ligation means I can't get pregnant, yet I still have hormone cycles. *Technically fertile.* There is no protection for me. "What if neither of those are an option?" I say hoarsely. "You know I can't have kids anymore."

"Yes." She takes my hand. "We've all agreed to set up a watch, and Erud will dig burrows women can sleep in for extra protection."

"Dens," the Fogarian corrects. "I would never relegate a female to a mere burrow."

Much as I appreciate his attempt to redefine comfort, a burrow or den sounds like fucking hell. I'm still processing everything when Jennifer moves over to join us. "I think I can get a signal out," she says. "But we need to take the beacon as high in the trees as possible."

Nazhin gets to his feet behind her and shakes out a massive pair of bat wings. I only recognize it's him because he still has a bald head and silvery eyes. He's sprouted a crown of small horns, and a long tail twitches behind him.

"Do any of you have experience flying?" he asks, flapping his wings once and lifting slightly off the ground.

"No, but I'll try if it means a chance for Suzanne to escape this planet." Kiozhi climbs wearily to his feet. He's been silent during the discussion about the parasite, but he's rubbing the back of his neck as if agitated.

"No need. I was just hoping for advice," Nazhin says. "You stay and protect the camp."

Everyone watches Nazhin practice flapping around above the camp, shouting advice while Kiozhi and I remain near the fire, finishing our food. My attention keeps drifting to his bandaged leg. He's injured because of me and Beanie. If I remain in camp, I'm a risk to him and everyone nearby. The last thing I want is someone dying while defending me. I look toward the wall of brush surrounding the camp, realizing that I only have one choice. One thing I can do to keep my sisters and the others safe.

I have to leave.

15

KIOZHI

I watch the expressions flit across Suzanne's face, my *Iki'i* reeling under her rapidly cycling emotions. Anxiety, uncertainty, despair.

My own feelings mimic hers. This parasite sounds formidable. "Don't worry. I'll die before I let anything hurt you."

Her shoulders are hunched, and she has a sadness in her eyes that cuts me to the core. "That's what I'm afraid of."

Shame fills me, but she has reason to doubt. I couldn't even overcome a carnivorous plant without losing part of my matrix. "I'll be on better alert. I promise."

She smiles tightly and turns her attention to Nazhin, who's careening above the clearing with ungainly flaps of his wings. If I was stronger, I'd join him as backup

106

for this rescue plan. I've never tried to assume a flying form before, but I understand how awkward it can be learning to use unfamiliar muscles and limbs.

Once he seems to get the hang of things, Jennifer and Nazhin leave for the treetops with the beacon. The rest of us settle around the fire with more food. Tamara and Suzanne chat about what's happened so far, but I'm too exhausted to keep up. My eyelids drift closed.

When I wake, Suzanne is no longer beside me. Hanzhu and Erud are also gone, and Tamara and Tazhio are asleep, snuggled together on the other side of the fire with Beanie curled contentedly against Tamara's belly. Only Ubi is awake, cooking something yellow and rubbery-looking jabbed on the end of a stick over the flames.

"Did you see where Suzanne went?" I ask the Hage crewman.

"I believe she followed Hanzhu and Erud." He pulls the stick toward him, pokes a finger at the yellow lump, then returns it to cooking. "They went to gather firewood."

I look toward the surrounding brush. Is Suzanne considering a mate other than me? My stomach feels full of acid. It would make sense for her to choose someone who isn't injured to protect her.

I pull the bandage from my leg. My skin looks less raw, and I don't think I need the covering anymore, but when I stand, I still feel weaker than I should. Though my stomach is roiling with uncertainty, I grab a handful of the starchy white stems; more nourishment will help me recover. "Which way did they go?"

Ubi points toward a narrow gap next to some glowing violet bushes with round leaves. "If you find any more of these mushrooms, please bring them back." He pulls the yellow lump from his stick and shoves it into his small mouth, speaking around his bulging cheeks. "They are quite satisfying."

The last thing I'm thinking about is mushroom hunting, but I nod and head toward the trail. I haven't traveled very far before I meet Hanzhu and Erud returning with armloads of wood. I scan the forest beyond them. "Where's Suzanne?"

Hanzhu tilts his head. "We haven't seen her."

My heart thumps harder against my ribs. "Ubi said she followed you."

Erud drops his sticks, hopefulness lighting his features. "She did?" He turns to look around the glowing brush. "We did not encounter her."

I release a shaky breath. I have a sneaking suspicion Suzanne didn't go in search of either of these males.

And if she's lost, it's because she wants to be. I turn in a slow circle, searching for any sign of her. She could be anywhere in this vast forest.

"Go back and tell the others she's missing," I say. "I'm going to look for her."

"Going alone isn't—" Hanzhu begins, but I cut him off.

"I'm aware of the dangers. Go tell the others." The longer I delay, the farther away Suzanne gets.

They sigh and hurry back to camp. I step up onto one of the many root paths snaking through the understory. If I were her, I'd try to go back to the cave with the spring in it. She marked our path with her waxy pink stick. If I can find the spot where we met her sisters, I should be able to pick up the trail.

I wander over the roots and through the bushes. Everything looks too similar. Then I see a trampled area I'm pretty sure was where the sisters stood hugging. I pick up the pace, finding Suzanne's color stick wedged in a V between two roots. When I unscrew the cap, it's empty.

She must have used it all to mark her way to this spot. I closely scan the nearby brush. *There.* A pale pink smudge is barely discernible on the purplish bark of a tree trunk ahead. All I have to do is look for the next mark.

Now that I know what I'm looking for, I reach the turquoise vines covering the entrance to the cave easily. Standing outside, I call softly, "Suzanne?"

Her pale face appears between the foliage, and alarm flicks my *Iki'i*. "What are you doing here?" she asks.

I push the vines aside and drop down next to her. "The better question is, what are you doing here?"

"You know what I'm doing. I'm a liability. A danger. You need to go back."

I move to the spring and kneel for a drink. "Nope."

"Kiozhi, I can't ask you to risk yourself for me."

"You're not." Moving over to the far wall, I plop down on the thick leaves with my back against the velvety moss. "Come, sit with me."

She hesitates, but then shakes her head and moves toward me. "You're an idiot, you know that?"

"Possibly." I smile wryly. "But I already lost one mate. I refuse to lose another."

She stops mid-step and stares at me. "What do you mean, you lost a mate?"

Talking about Nanaia is still painful, but if I ever hope to have Suzanne in my life, I have to be open with her. "She died in a collision. An intoxicated driver had turned off the guidance system in his vehicle. Neither of them survived."

I've imagined her death a million times, and the weight of it presses in on me again now. I only realize how tightly my fingers are clenched when Suzanne's soft fingers slide over my knuckles. "I'm so sorry. What was her name?"

"Nanaia." Saying her name out loud seems to release a dam inside me, and I keep talking, turning my hand up to lace my fingers with Suzanne's. "Kirenai mate for life, and after she died, I thought I was doomed to a long, lonely existence knowing what joy was but never finding it again. I spent tens of cycles in therapy, tried to find purpose in building my investments, even turned to pleasures of the flesh in an attempt to feel something besides pain. People called me a playboy, but inside I was dying every day." I lift my eyes to meet Suzanne's face and see her green eyes glazed with tears. My own eyes prickle, and I lift my free hand and cup her cheek. "Then I heard you laugh at the party, and it was like I'd just been rescued from a black hole."

Her fingers tighten around mine, and I watch her swallow. "Don't put that burden on me, Kiozhi. Please." There is pain in her eyes. "I have my own baggage. Half my life has already been lost chained to someone else's needs. I can't save you."

I gently stroke her cheek with my thumb. "You already saved me. And I have no desire to put you in chains. But I will always choose to remain near you in whatever capacity you'll allow."

Emotions play out on her face, her indecision like a thousand tiny wings beating against my *Iki'i*. Her eyes dart from my eyes to my mouth and back before she swallows hard and answers. "I'm not done exploring what it means to be me. What if I want to see other men?"

Jealousy flares in my chest, crowding out all other emotions. *She doesn't understand the mate bond.* "If we become mates, neither of us will want another person. That's how the mate bond works."

"But if I do?" she insists.

I run my tongue over the front of my teeth thoughtfully. Then I lean closer until we share the same breath. "Tell you what. If I ever fail to measure up to your expectations, then you can seek affection elsewhere."

She narrows her eyes, a smile quirking her lips. "Really? Because I'll hold you to that."

A matching smile twists the corner of my mouth. "You have my vow."

She shakes her head. "I must be an idiot. But..." Sighing, she leans forward and seals that vow with a kiss.

113

16

SUZANNE

Kiozhi's mouth on mine feels like something out of a dream, surreal and too good to be true. I have no idea if this arrangement will work, but he pushes all the right buttons to make me crave him. We've made love before, but right now, I want to melt into him. To become one with him in a way I've never felt before. I don't want to admit it, but the idea of being his and his alone feeds something inside me I didn't know was hungry.

His tongue slides over my lips, parting me to his caress as his fingers move to my neck, holding me close.

I moan softly into his mouth. "Why do I want you so much, Kiozhi?"

He kisses the corner of my mouth, then slides his lips down the column of my throat, sending shivers of delight through my center. "Because I belong to you. Weren't you listening?"

We sink to the leafy floor of the cave, our bodies pressed close together as he runs his hands over my body. He lifts my shirt and bra, taking a nipple into his mouth. It tightens at his touch, and I whimper softly, arching up as he nips and sucks one breast before moving to the other.

Kissing his way down my stomach, he kneels between my legs, removing my pants and panties. His hands roam up between my thighs to stroke the outer folds of my pussy. I shudder and widen my legs, yearning to feel him inside me. He dips a finger into my channel, and I groan, tightening around him. He finds my G-spot with practiced ease, stroking with increasing intensity as I writhe. Before I tip over the edge into orgasm, he pulls free and replaces his finger with the thickness of his cock.

I gasp and buck up to meet him, my orgasm exploding like fireworks behind my eyes. He stays there, pulsing inside me, but I don't think he came yet.

Lowering himself to cover me, he holds me tight and begins to thrust again, building me into another frenzy. We move together, our bodies slick with sweat and lust. Something prods my ass, and he growls against my ear, "Are you ready, *kikajiru?*"

I'm gasping, Kiozhi's cock deep in my body, the beginning of another climax thrumming through my veins. "God, yes!"

I wrap my heels behind his ass, pulling him closer. I'm so wet, there's little resistance, just sensation as he penetrates and fills me. The double sensation tips me over the edge and I scream, back arching in ultimate pleasure.

He pounds into me, driving my climax to impossible heights. Then he bellows and thrusts forward, filling me with heated jets of his seed.

Collapsing above me, elbows supporting the bulk of his weight, he breathes against the side of my neck. My heels are still locked behind him, and I loosen their hold, letting my legs fall like lead weights to either side. Limp and boneless, we lay there together, simply soaking up each other's essence.

I kiss the warm skin of his shoulder, tasting his salt. "That was... different than before."

"Better, I hope?" He rolls off me and pulls me over onto his chest.

I nod against his skin, trying to process all the feelings inside me. I hadn't really believed him when he said the mate bond would change me. Sex and love had always been something I wanted to be synonymous, but until this moment, I didn't understand exactly what that might feel like. Now I do. It's like a blanket fresh from the dryer, warm and irresistible. Or having someone hand you comfort food after a stressful day. A perfect sensation I will now crave forever.

"Will it always feel this way?" I ask.

"Yes." His voice rumbles under my cheek. "We are true bonded mates. You are my everything. I love you, *kikajiru.*"

I'm dizzy with the knowledge of his words. In a whisper, I reply, "I love you too."

We rest and make love again before Kiozhi convinces me he should let my sisters know I'm okay. I'm worried they will insist on dragging me back, but he promises he won't let that happen. I sit with my back against the wall facing the entrance, a makeshift spear at my side. If something tries to get in, I want to be ready. While I wait, I think about my girls, my parents, my other sister, Bethany, who's still on the *Romantasy*. Will I ever see any of them again? Am I going to spend the rest of my existence basically trapped in this cave on an alien planet?

By the time Kiozhi returns, I'm teary-eyed with a full-on pity party.

He pads over and sits down next to me. "Everything okay?"

I nod and swipe angrily at my cheeks. "How'd my sisters take it?"

"They're not happy," he says, "but they believe me when I tell them you're alive."

"Did Jennifer set up the beacon?"

"Yes. Now all we can do is wait. I'll check back every day to see if a rescue ship has arrived."

I sigh and lean my head on his shoulder. "I'm already out of my mind with boredom."

He puts a hand on my knee and slides it up the inside of my thigh. In a low voice, he says, "I can think of a few things to keep you occupied."

17

KIOZHI

We fall into a routine of me going to the camp while Suzanne remains in the cave. Food and rest have brought my strength back, though regenerating my full matrix will take longer. We have no way of knowing day from night, and I don't know how much time passes this way. There is no talk of the future. We just live in the present.

At the camp, I learn what plants are edible, and though I'd prefer to gather them and bring them back to Suzanne, she insists she'll go crazy if she's cooped up in the cave all the time. I grudgingly agree she can accompany me to forage, but we both carry sharpened sticks with us.

We've just finished gathering purple fruits when she runs her fingers over the thick, toothy spike of a flaming orange plant. "This is shaped exactly like an aloe plant from Earth." She glances around. "I wonder how many of these plants might have medical uses? I wish I had a notebook or something so I could keep a record."

"You could use my ICC." I lift my arm and bring up the interface. "I'll have to operate it, but just tell me what to record and when we get back to the ship, we'll transfer it to your media."

Her eyes light up. "That would be amazing."

I show her how to run the interface and then hold my arm steady so she can document the plant. She uses both hands on my arm to aim the camera implant, her hair covering part of her cheek as she takes the picture. She moves us around the plant, positioning my arm for each individual picture, then breaks off the tip of one spike, photographing the inside. "Too bad we can't preserve actual samples."

A sibilant noise echoes between the trees, and she jerks her head up and looks around. "Was that my name?"

"I'm not sure." I scan the depths of the dim forest with my *Iki'i* but can't detect anyone.

"Sussssuuunnnn." The sound comes again.

A prickle races along my spine. I drop my arm, letting my ICC go dark. "I don't think that's human. We need to go back to the cave."

We both grab our spears and retrace our steps, but before we've taken twenty paces, a woman's scream splits the air. Suzanne spins around and looks at me with wide eyes. "That was human."

I grit my teeth. I already know she's going to argue that we need to go help. "We don't know that for sure."

"It was. And if it was me out there in trouble, you'd want someone to help, right?" She turns back toward the sound.

"*Kuzara*," I grumble. "At least stay behind me, okay?"

We cautiously make our way through the forest toward the sound. The screaming continues, accompanied by the sibilant buzz and some strange chittering.

Skirting the base of a tree, we emerge on a scene that makes my jaw drop. Six or eight furry bipeds with banded purple fur are locked in battle with a flying creature that's larger than I am. The creature has one biped trapped in its long legs and is trying to lift the kicking, screeching being from the ground. The sound of Suzanne's name is coming from its flapping, gossamer green wings.

"I think those furry beings are Sheeghr," I whisper, grabbing Suzanne's arm to pull her back out of sight. I've never met the local tribe, but these beings match the descriptions Tamara and Tazhio gave us.

The Sheeghr on the ground clutch their captured comrade's limbs and stab the flying creature with crude spears.

"Look, in the middle," Suzanne whispers.

A human female with golden brown hair huddles on her hands and knees in the center of the commotion, trying not to get trampled or stabbed. It looks like her hands and feet are tied.

"We have to help." Suzanne steps forward. "They're going to kill her."

One of the Sheeghr spots Suzanne's movement and looks straight at us. He chitters something in a language my universal translator doesn't understand. My *Iki'i* can't decipher any emotions beyond the maelstrom of hostility, but I think he may be asking for help. I frown at the bound woman in their midst but recognize now isn't the time for questions. She's in danger, and we need to help.

I grab Suzanne's arm and make her look at me. "Wait here. If things go wrong, promise you'll run back to the cave."

"I'm not—"

"I can't have my attention divided if I'm going to save that woman. Promise, or I take you back to the cave myself."

She scowls at me, but nods. "Fine."

Gritting my teeth, I raise my spear and move toward the fray, hardening my matrix so I don't get damaged—I've learned my lesson the hard way with the beasts on this planet.

The bound woman spots me, her cheeks dirty and stained with tears. "Oh, thank God! Help me, please!"

I'm a head taller than the Sheeghr, but the winged creature is still barely within my reach. I pull back my arm and hurl my spear. It bounces uselessly off the creature's carapace, but the impact distracts it enough to let the pack drag their friend from its grip.

The flying creature rises, obviously posed to strike again. Then, as if changing its mind, it swivels.

And heads straight for Suzanne.

Her eyes widen, and she spins, tripping through the brush to get away.

I pelt after them, weaponless and furious. I knew it was a mistake to leave her side. Sheeghr race past me, bounding forward on all fours. But the winged creature is faster. It catches up to Suzanne, long pointed legs stretching down to grab her.

She screams and drops to the ground. The beast zooms past over her head, feet brushing the leaves along the trail. Suzanne scrambles upright and turns back toward us, running for all she's worth. Behind her, the winged creature has veered around and is coming back for her.

The pack shrieks and chitters, already circling up around her. By the time I reach them, one of them has dragged the other woman along, and she lays curled in a ball on the ground, sobbing. They lob more yellow stones into the air. The winged beast weaves and sways, its flight looking drunken under the onslaught, but it persists in coming forward.

It catches hold of another biped and successfully takes to the air. But instead of flying away, it rises several stories into the air and drops the screaming Sheeghr. The being's screams are cut short on impact with the ground.

Suzanne gasps beside me.

The beast buzzes around and dive-bombs us again. There is no stopping this thing, not until it gets what it wants, which appears to be the women. It's going to pick us off one-by-one if we don't find a way to bring it down first.

I plant my feet wide and wait for the next time it approaches. If I can just get hold of a leg or two, I might be able to use its own momentum against it. Suzanne stands next to me, spear gripped in both hands. "I'm going to try to drag it toward me," I say. "Be ready."

The creature swings a crooked path overhead, dodging yellow missiles. But eventually, it comes within reach, aiming for Suzanne. The moment it's in range, I grab its legs and yank downward.

At the same moment, Suzanne lets out a feral scream and jabs upward with her spear. The pointed tip skitters over the carapace before lodging in the crevice between its thorax and abdomen. The creature lets out a horrible grating noise, its momentum driving the shaft deep into its body. It careens into Suzanne, laying her out flat on the forest floor.

"Suzanne!" I grab the creature by a spasming wing and heave it off her.

Suzanne is looking up at the sky with unblinking eyes. A trickle of crimson blood drips from her nose, bright against her ashen skin. I kneel next to her, my heart refusing to beat. She can't die. Surely fate wouldn't be this cruel. "Suzanne?"

She blinks slowly. "Is it dead?"

Heart jolted back into rhythm, I laugh and gather her into my arms. "Yes, my love. The beast is dead."

Her fingers claw against my chest, her gaze turning toward the surrounding Sheeghr. "Now what about them?"

I glance up and realize the Sheeghr are all leering at us. And every one of them has a prominent pink phallus poking from between his legs.

18

SUZANNE

Muscles tense, I glance beyond the surrounding Sheeghr toward where the blonde woman remains huddled on the ground. She's sobbing incoherently. "Untie her," I demand.

The Sheeghr purr and chitter, but make no move toward the woman. They seem to have completely forgotten her now that I'm here. My stomach roils when one of them grabs his dick and brandishes it toward me.

Kiozhi lets go of me and stands, surprisingly unaggressive. His modesty shield is gone, revealing a huge blue erection jutting like a shelf from his crotch. "I'm fairly certain they mean no harm," he says without looking at me. "Your sister said the Sheeghr establish status based on the size of their penises."

To my utter surprise, the Sheeghr turn away as if satisfied by his show of masculinity. They move to their fallen friend, emitting small, high-pitched squeaks as they arrange his body.

I feel sorry for them, but I'm more worried about the woman. Climbing unsteadily to my feet, I stumble to her and fall to my knees I try prying apart the knots around her ankles, but my hands tremble, and I can't seem to get a decent grip on the vine.

"Let me," Kiozhi says, taking over.

I glance at the Sheeghr. Several are now carrying their friend away into the brush, while the rest have begun slicing the downed creature into pieces with crude knives. One of them tucks the severed wings into a pack on his back, the gossamer green blades fanning above his head like an otherworldly peacock's tail.

A shudder rolls through me. The beast looks a lot like a giant dragonfly. I might've even considered it pretty if it hadn't been attacking us. Turning back to the woman, I realize how young she is—not much older than my daughters. "What's your name, honey?" I ask.

"A-amy," she says between sobs. "Those ferret aliens threatened to rape me. When I fought back, they hog-tied me like a dead animal. Then that flying thing attacked—" she chokes and throws her arms around me. "I thought I was the only one from the shuttle left alive."

I cringe, feeling all my new bruises. "It's okay." I stroke her hair and give her a squeeze, feeling homesick for my children. "That creature is dead. You're safe now."

Not that I believe my own words. That flying thing had to be the parasite, and I'm not sure we could've killed it without the help of the Sheeghr.

The furry aliens appear to be arguing over the monster, showing off their penises to each other. One turns toward Kiozhi, as if inviting him to take part, and I realize Kiozhi remains standing on full display. He purrs back, and the Sheeghr turns away.

Amy is gawking at him, and he turns so his back is to her.

I smile appreciatively. *That's my guy.*

Several of the Sheeghr approach carrying body parts. They bow and chitter, offering dripping bits to me and Amy.

Amy buries her face against my shoulder. I shake my head and hold her tighter. "No, thank you."

Kiozhi says something that sends them away, then looks over his shoulder at us. "They want to escort us back to the survivor camp."

"You can understand them?" Amy asks.

"Just a few words," he says. "They call themselves Sheeghr, and others in camp have interacted with them."

I'm less concerned about understanding the Sheeghr and more about returning to camp. "I can't go back to camp. That parasite was definitely attracted to me."

Kiozhi shrugs. "The Sheeghr aren't going to let us traipse off alone. I think we have to go with them, at least for now. "

I count five Sheeghr still with us. I doubt we can run and hide from them. With a resigned sigh, I stand and help Amy to her feet. My adrenaline rush is fading, and my muscles feel weak as we follow the Sheeghr through the brush. I can't breathe through my nose, and when I lift my fingers to my upper lip, they come away sticky with blood.

Thankfully, we don't have to walk too far before a familiar barking greets us and Beanie comes racing out to greet us. The tiny dog dances around Kiozhi, insisting on being picked up.

"Still best buds, I see." I smirk at him.

He just smiles back and rubs Beanie's head before setting him back on the ground.

The Sheeghr seem in awe of the little dog, muttering among themselves and keeping a respectful distance. I hear my sister calling for him, and a moment later, Tamara appears. She rushes forward. "Suzanne!" She halts and gives me a startled once-over. "You look like you've been through hell."

"You have no idea," I say, wiping dried blood from under my nose.

The Sheeghr insist on leading us all the way back to camp, where Erud and Hanzhu fawn over Amy. While the Sheeghr engage in a chittering conversation with Tamara and Tazhio. I glance over the assembled people, noting that the camp has grown. There are at least fourteen survivors here now, including another human woman.

"How many people are still missing?" I ask Jennifer.

"According to Ubi, this is everyone."

"No sign of a rescue?" I ask, glancing upward as if a shuttle might magically appear.

She shrugs. "We won't know until one arrives. All we can do is be ready."

I press my lips together and nod, but a sick feeling has settled in my stomach. It's been days since she set the beacon, and even more since the crash. If rescue teams haven't figured out where we are by now, I doubt they ever will.

Kiozhi puts an arm around my shoulders and guides me toward the fire where Erud is twisting open a purple fruit for Amy. It looks like she's already eaten one or two based on the discarded hulls in front of her, and she listens with rapt attention as Erud talks to her.

I'd prefer to leave, but doubt I'll be allowed while the Sheeghr are still hanging around, so I sit. Jennifer offers me a leaf that's been folded into a cup. It contains water, and I suck it down gratefully. It tastes musty and herbal, nothing like the fresh water from our cave, but I'm grateful.

"How are you?" Kiozhi asks, dabbing at my chin with a scrap of damp cloth.

"My nose is throbbing, but I'm okay." I take the cloth and scrub my upper lip. What I wouldn't do for some ice right now.

Tamara and Tazhio us, and I glance toward where the Sheeghr are departing into the trees. "That thing you fought was a Gloor," Tazhio says. "The Sheeghr's name for the parasite. I guess defeating it was quite an accomplishment."

"Yeah, we were lucky." I glance toward the sky.

Tamara nudges me with an elbow. "They were impressed that you killed it. I hope you don't mind we let them keep all the trophies."

I'm in no mood for humor, though. "I need to leave." I stand and look at Kiozhi expectantly. "The longer I stay, the higher chance I might draw another of those things."

"Wait," says Jennifer, moving to stand in front of me. "Amy says she has an IUD."

I frown. "So?"

"Like you, she's fertile but can't get pregnant."

The thought of another person joining me and Kiozhi in the cave sounds unpleasant—not to mention we'll lose the privacy we've been enjoying—but what else can I do? "She can come with us."

"I'm not going anywhere," Amy says. Her hair's tangled and her skin and clothes are so dirty I can't even tell what color they're supposed to be. "The rescue is coming here, so this is where I'm staying."

I scowl at her. "You saw how dangerous the parasite is. If you stay, you'll just draw another one to the camp and get everyone killed."

She looks around at the assembled survivors. "There are enough of us here to fight it off."

"One of the Sheeghr died protecting you," I remind her. "Are you willing to let more people die like that?"

"Going off alone only divides our forces." She takes one of Erud's clawed hands. "The more people we have to fight, the better chance we have to survive. Right, Erud?"

His red mustache curls up into a grin. "I will keep you safe no matter what."

Kiozhi puts one hand on my knee. "They're right. There is strength in numbers."

"Staying is irresponsible," I say, pressing my mouth into a hard line. I can't believe he's taking their side.

His gaze is soft, and he squeezes my knee gently. "Suzanne, it's time you allow others to share responsibility. You don't need to be the one always sacrificing yourself to take care of someone else."

I ponder that for a moment, thinking about all the times I've bemoaned my responsibilities. Taken on everything myself so that others weren't inconvenienced. "This is different," I insist. "This is literally life or death."

"Doesn't that make it even more important?" He raises his eyebrows. "What would you do if one of your sisters was in your place?"

Dammit. It's not fair that he's right. I chew my lip, then huff, "Fine."

Tamara leans over and hugs me, and Jennifer comes over to squeeze me from behind. I lean into them with my eyes closed, praying, *God, please don't let me doom them all to a horrible death.*

19

SUZANNE

"I feel like an unwilling contestant on a reality TV show," I complain, picking at a splinter in my thumb. I'm trying to weave a basket out of vines while Jennifer fiddles with electronics salvaged from the shuttle. "I'm just waiting to be voted off."

Jennifer snorts. "If only it was that easy. That would mean you get to go home."

I glance upward for the billionth time since agreeing to stay in camp, listening for the whisper of wings through the trees. Wisps of pale smoke float lazily through the darkness from the leaves we're burning to keep the Gloor away. The entire camp smells like burning socks, but I'm not sure the smoke is working. Twice now Amy and I have fled to one of Erud's tiny burrows when a shadowy form was spotted above the camp.

Despite everything we're doing, I'm not sure Amy and I should stay. There are so many people I care about here, people who are in danger because of me. And with Tamara pregnant, she counts as two. Kiozhi and I were doing well on our own—

Kiozhi plops down beside me. "Don't even think about it."

I glare at him. I both hate and love that he knows me so well. "You're really annoying, you know that?"

He just smirks in response and cracks open a purple fruit, offering me half. I decline, returning to my basket weaving.

"Is she thinking of running away again?" Jennifer asks.

Irritated that she's talking about me like I'm not listening, I say, "I'm right here, you know."

"I know," Jennifer says with a smile. "But sometimes your selflessness is actually a little selfish."

My blood heats with ire, and I thrust my basket aside. How dare she call me selfish? Even before I had kids of my own I was helping Mom take care of my three younger sisters. "What the hell is that supposed to mean? I've given everything for the people I love."

She lowers the nest of wires she's holding to her lap. "Yes, you have. Even when you shouldn't. And I'm not saying it's unappreciated. But accepting from others can be a gift, too."

I clench my teeth about to retort, but Jennifer thrusts her palm out. "Just listen. Remember when you were in the hospital after your appendix burst? You were in so much pain and scared out of your mind. Mom and I were by your side the whole time, but we couldn't do anything to help you. All we could do was watch as you suffered."

"Yeah, I remember." I lower my head, feeling the weight of those memories bearing down on me. Mom missed her vacation because of me.

"Then when you were discharged, you refused to let us come home with you, even though the nurses said you would need someone to help. You pushed us away and insisted on going through it alone. And I get why you did. You're strong and independent, and you didn't want to burden us. But it took you three months to recover when it should've only taken one."

My throat constricts, and I have to swallow hard before I can speak. "I hate feeling weak and helpless. I also hate letting others see that side of me."

She nods solemnly. "I know. And it's okay to not want to show your vulnerable side to others. But you need to realize that you can't do everything yourself. We're family, and we all help each other no matter what. We can help you stay alive on this planet."

"It's different—"

"Is it? Or is it even more vital we act as a team?" Jennifer spears me with her gaze. "You're not the only one allowed to sacrifice for someone. How do you think we'll feel if you die out there all alone? We'll always wonder if there was something we could've done to save you. Or what if something else attacks the camp and we need your help to fight it off?"

I press my lips together and stare at the uneven weave on my basket. "God dammit," I mutter. She's right. Yet how can I surrender my fear? If they die because of me, I may as well die, too.

Kiozhi takes my hands. "I know you're scared," he says gently. "But asking for help from others can be a strength, not a weakness, and our forces help them as much as they help us."

My heart aches but I nod, squeezing his hand back. "I just hope a rescue arrives soon."

Nazhin joins us, settling next to Jennifer. One of his huge wings circles protectively around her back and he poked a clawed finger at the wires in her lap. "Find anything useful?"

"Not yet," she says, picking up the tangle.

I tilt my head, examining the horns on his forehead. I thought Kirenai are supposed to look like a member of their mate's species once they bond, but although he and Jennifer say they're mated, he's definitely not human. "Nazhin, why do you still look Khargal?"

He shrugs. "I haven't tried to shift back to human yet because we might need my wings."

Jennifer gives Nazhin a sly wink. "Plus, I find this form sexy."

He smiles at her, his silver eyes glinting. "Oh, really?"

I roll my eyes, but I'm also smiling. I enjoy seeing my sisters with mates they obviously adore and who adore them back. My attention slides over to Kiozhi to find him smiling softly at me. I'm about to say something when a throaty buzzing interrupts me from the trees. *Sussshuuu sussshuuu.*

I jump to my feet, heart about to explode. This doesn't sound like one Gloor coming in to attack.

It sounds like an entire flock.

KIOZHI

Suzanne darts toward one of the dens, shouting, "Are we under attack?"

I stand, searching the sky and poised for action. The sound isn't like the Gloor's wings. It's more powerful, a grumble rather than a buzz. I know that sound.

"It's a shuttle!" Tazhio shouts. "Come on!"

The entire camp surges into motion. I dart after Suzanne and grab her hand, keeping pace with the others as we hurry through the dense forest with our eyes on the canopy. Something sounds like it's crashing through branches far overhead, and the rumbling is growing louder.

Branches and leaves start raining down on us, and bright green light spears down from the sky. A fierce wind rips down through the trees. We crowd up near the base of a trunk, trying to avoid getting hit by debris. Overhead, I spot a shuttle coming in fast, engines straining as it dodges the largest of the limbs.

"We're saved!" someone shouts.

I'm not so sure. The vessel wobbles, and for a moment, I think it's going to retreat, then it drops with a heavy thud to the forest floor.

A cheer rises from the group, and everyone rushes forward, cowering as debris continues to fall from above. The wind drives leaves and branches against us, and Suzanne's hair whips around her face like it has a life of its own. Ahead of us, Nazhin raises a wing over Jennifer like an umbrella. I envy his ability, but I'm still recovering from the loss of my matrix, and holding a human form has been challenge enough.

The shuttle's purple hull is scratched and dented, and the pointed nose is bent to one side. I'm impressed it's in one piece. Its hatch rolls open, and a brown spiny G'nax in a dark blue uniform stumbles out onto the ramp. Yellow blood stains the collar of his uniform.

Tazhio reaches the ramp first. "Eraj! I should've known you'd be the one to come for us."

Eraj is clutching a small box in one hand. "We received your transmission." He staggers and Tazhio offers a supportive shoulder. Gesturing toward the green light spearing down through the trees, Eraj continues, "I used the first available window through the storm, but I'm afraid the shuttle took some damage. We need to go before the window closes, but I'm not sure I can fly."

The branches overhead are whipping like tentacles, and it's hard to take a full breath in the blasting wind. I lean into it, trying to provide a shield for Suzanne against the brunt of the storm. Streaks of angry red and purple arc down from the green sky.

Tazhio motions to two people from camp. "Take him in and see to his injuries. The rest of you, on board now." He grins. "I'm flying us home."

Clutching Suzanne's hand, I scramble up the ramp with the others. This isn't a luxury shuttle with plush seats that transform into safety pods. It's a military ship with basic personnel harnesses lining the walls. I strap Suzanne in before taking the spot next to her.

The ramp rolls closed, leaving us in near darkness except for the dim glow through a pair of viewports near the door to the cockpit. At least we're now sheltered from the wind. We all wait in silence, the sour stink of fear filling the cabin.

"Are we going to take off?" Amy asks, both arms clutched over the straps on her chest.

A few minutes later, the shuttle deck hums and gravity tilts as we wobble up off the ground. We jerk sideways then shoot upward.

From the cockpit, I hear, "Waaahooo!"

I stare that direction, praying my friend really is as good a pilot as he always claims to be.

It feels like we're spinning, and the floor shakes until my teeth are rattling. The light from the viewports shifts from sickly green to a vibrant yellow. A moan courses through the ship, rising in pitch until it sounds like an opera soprano. Pink sparkles fill the air, coalescing into globs that drift and flow like drops of water in zero gravity. Then the turbulence stops.

I lean forward, trying to see through one of the small viewports. It looks dark. Someone is sobbing, and another person whispers, "He did it."

My heart fills with hope. I stretch my hand out and take Suzanne's. A disbelieving smile lights her features. Across the cabin from us, Jennifer is grinning like a fool, her hand gripping Nazhin's. "My beacon worked!"

SUZANNE

We step off the shuttle onto a dull gray deck full of armed guards in dark blue uniforms. "This isn't the *Romantasy*," I say, clutching Kiozhi's hands. "What's going on?" I can't help thinking of all the sci-fi movies I've seen where people end up on dissection tables after being exposed to alien pathogens.

He squeezes my fingers. "Guess they brought out the big guns to find us. These are imperial soldiers."

I gulp. "Are they afraid we're dangerous or something?"

"I don't know." He draws me closer to his side as we're escorted down a nondescript hallway.

The entire group of survivors shuffle into what appears to be a medical facility, much like the ones I've seen in Sci-Fi movies. There's an exam table and a few beds, and everything's made of metal. The walls are a shiny silver color and the machines and equipment stand like vaguely threatening sentries. The doctor is a bright pink alien who reminds me of a monitor lizard wearing a long black skirt held up by suspenders.

"My name is Dr. Egwan," he says in a soft, nasal voice. "I'll be seeing to your health before we transport you back to the *Romantasy* for your journey home. Who would like to go first? Are any of you injured?"

I'm actually surprised at how few of us are hurt. After more than a week stranded on that hostile planet and all the creatures we fought off, you'd think we'd be in worse shape.

I push Kiozhi forward. "Have your matrix checked."

"But your nose—"

I shake my head. "Is nothing compared to what you suffered. Go."

Sighing, he follows the doctor into another room. While the rest of us wait our turns, a crew member offers us nutrient bars. They taste like cardboard but might as well be ambrosia as I wolf mine down.

Kiozhi comes out and I push Tamara forward. "Go get that baby checked out. I want to know how Kiozhi's exam went."

She nods gratefully and takes Tazhio's hand. "Come with me."

They follow the doctor, and I had Kiozhi a nutrient bar. "How'd it go?"

He tears open the package. "He offered me time in a regeneration pod, but I prefer waiting until we get back to the *Romantasy*. It'll take a day or two for full recovery, and I don't want to keep us stuck on this ship."

"Which of you is the owner of Demod Industries?" someone calls. A slender alien with skin white as snow and raven hair braided in several rows over her head stands at the med bay door.

Nazhin steps forward, still in Khargal form. "That'd be me."

"We assume you're the one who sent a signal from the surface," the slender alien says. "Nice job. We'd like to have a chat with you once you're done here."

"It wasn't me." Nazhin takes Jennifer's hand and pulls her beside him. "It was Jennifer."

My sister is smiling so broadly, I swear every one of her teeth show. She extends her hand toward the woman. "Jennifer Bloom."

The woman tilts her head as if confused, then takes Jennifer's hand. "A human? Now I'm even more intrigued. Are you willing to discuss this technology with us?"

"Is the Confederation willing to lift restrictions on sharing technology with Earth?" Jennifer asks.

"Ah." The woman bows her head respectfully. "A wise question. I believe the Senburu will consider it. But I will verify before we proceed."

"Thank you," says Jennifer.

The woman leaves, and my sister shoots me a satisfied smirk.

"Well played," I say, smiling back.

"I know, right?"

Tamara emerges from the exam room holding Tazhio's hand. Beanie trots beside her, the missing fur on his rump now fully restored. She joins us, looking somewhat shocked.

"Is everything okay?" I ask.

She nods, a dumbfounded smile on her face. "I—"

"We've just been told we're going to have twins!" Tazhio puts an arm around her shoulders. He's grinning as he looks at Kiozhi. "Can you believe it? Twins!"

I blink for a moment. For some reason, Tamara's pregnancy never seemed real to me. It seemed impossible in such a short time. But I guess a lot of impossible has happened to us on this trip. I laugh and wink at Tazhio. "Twins run in our family. Boy, are you in for a ride."

Tamara smiles nervously. "And one is a boy, so he'll be a shapeshifter. I'm going to need all the help I can get."

"You know I'm always here for you." I hug my sister.

"Me too." Jennifer joins the hug. "But I'm handing them back if they get fussy."

Kiozhi pushes me toward the doctor. "You're next."

I follow him to a small room off the main medical bay. Panels on the walls scroll with green alien symbols. The plain metal exam table hovers in midair.

"Lie down here please," the doctor instructs.

I'm not sure what to expect, but at least he didn't ask me to undress, so I don't think it will include any awkward probing. I lay back on the hard metal while he waves a handheld scanner over me from head to toe.

"Can you do anything for my nose?" I ask. Though it no longer throbs, it's still stuffy, and I'd hate to have lasting damage.

"Of course," he says. "Let me look at your scan first."

He turns and reads the scrolling data on a nearby panel. I can't help staring at the scales on his bright pink tail. I've met so many aliens recently, but he's the first lizard-like one.

After a few minutes, he says, "Oh, dear."

I sit up, looking at the panels as if I'll suddenly be able to read them. I haven't seen myself in a mirror yet, but I suddenly worry my nose will be crooked forever. "Is it unfixable?"

"You have a minor blockage in your reproductive system."

Oh, shit. Bile rises into my throat as I imagine my stomach filled with parasite eggs. This is way worse than a bent nose. "What kind of blockage?"

He pulls the arm of a nearby machine toward me. "Scar tissue is preventing the passage of gametes into your gestational organ. An easy fix—"

"Wait!" I put up my hands to ward him off. My heart is beating too fast. I'm pretty sure he's talking about my tubal ligation. "That scar tissue is intentional. I don't want it fixed." When I'd requested the procedure all those years ago, the doctor had been a bit of an asshole, making me establish evidence that I really wanted the surgery, so I feel a need to add, "I already have two children."

His lizard face has no expression that I can read, though he tilts his head as if confused. "I see." He scratches under his chin. "Your scans show the genetic markers of a Kirenai mate bond. Is he aware of your condition?"

Kiozhi and I never talked about whether or not he wants children of his own. When I agreed to be his mate, it never came up. But he does know I can't get pregnant because it was the entire reason I had to stay away from the camp.

I nod firmly. "Yes, he is."

But my gut is churning as I return to the others and sit next to Kiozhi. What if he assumed I'd get the procedure reversed when we got back to civilization? The doctor made it sound like an effortless task. Now that we're no longer stranded on that planet, will Kiozhi try to convince me to have more kids? If I refuse, will he regret taking me as a mate? I swallow, realizing how wrecked I'll be if he does either of those things. But I raised two kids already. I sure as hell don't want to start all over again.

Sensing my mood, he puts an arm around me. "Is everything all right?"

I sigh and stare at my hands folded in my lap. "I'm worried you're going to regret taking me as a mate."

"Why would I regret it?"

I sit in silence for a moment before answering. "The doctor just offered to make me able to have more children."

He remains perfectly still. "I thought you didn't want more."

I turn to look at him. "I don't."

His features soften. "I promised I'd never ask of you anything you didn't freely offer."

"But don't you want kids?"

He cups my cheek. "I'm blessed enough to have you."

Relief makes me want to melt, and I wrap my arms around him, loving that he hugs me back tightly and without an ounce of doubt. "I love you, Kiozhi."

"And I love you, Suzanne. With every molecule of my matrix."

I grin. It took crash landing on an alien planet to find my perfect mate, but now I could never imagine life without him. I don't have a clue what that life is going to look like, but I'm totally going to rock this next adventure.

SUZANNE

*F*ull fanfare greets our return to the *Romantasy.* I think every passenger on board has crammed into the shuttle bay to see us, and a band plays a processional march as we stride across the red carpet to a raised platform. All I want to do is take a shower, call my kids, and fall asleep in an actual bed, but the captain insists on making a speech.

"Thank you all for coming to celebrate the safe return of fourteen of our esteemed guests." The captain is a spiny alien that reminds me of a bug. He stands behind a podium with his arms rigid against his sides, and the spines on his head move when he talks. "On behalf of the Intergalactic Dating Agency, I would like to offer you all free passage for life. And for those whose lives were lost, we will pay restitution to the families."

I frown, wondering if someone died trying to save us. If so, this is the first I'm hearing about it, and I think it's rather shitty to gloss over such a heroic loss. Sophia's death was dreadful enough, and thinking about how devastated her family will be makes my throat feel tight.

Thinking of family, I look for Bethany among the crowd. Why isn't she front and center, demanding to be let on stage to hug us? Perhaps the captain is insisting on making it part of this god-awful ceremony. I yawn, hoping it'll be over soon, and lean into Kiozhi.

The captain comes along the line of survivors on stage, making a strange alien salute to each person. When he reaches me and my sisters, he bows deeply. "I cannot adequately express my grief over your loss." He extends a green piece of plastic the size of a poker chip. "I know this cannot bring your sister back, but I hope it will help ease your pain."

I blink at him, unsure if it's exhaustion making me hear things or what. "Bring my sister back?" I look at Tamara and Jennifer, who appear to be just as confused as I am. "We're all here, though."

"I speak of Bethany. She didn't return with you."

"Of course not," I say. "She wasn't on the excursion with us." Nausea clenches my stomach, and I look out over the audience, shouting, "Bethany? Where are you? Come up here."

The audience murmurs, but my baby sister doesn't appear. Jennifer and Tamara move to the front of the platform and start calling into the crowd. "Bethany!"

My legs tremble and the roar of the crowd increases, people shouting Bethany's name to help locate her. Where is she?

The cruise director scrolls through a document on his ICC. "Her name is on the manifest," he says. "And she hasn't accessed her cabin or used any of the ship's amenities since your shuttle left. Is it possible you didn't realize she was on board with you?"

I round on him. "There were only fifteen fucking people on there. One of us would've noticed her."

"Ubi, you said all the passengers were accounted for, right?" Tamara asks, clutching Beanie against her chest.

The small alien looks frightened but nods. "Yes."

"She wasn't on the shuttle," Jennifer insists. "I would've seen her on my app."

I add, "She was too focused on getting that chef to join her cooking show to join us."

"Ch-chef?" the cruise director stutters. He turns to the captain. "Sir, one of our Kirenai chefs went missing around the same time as the shuttle crash. We've been unable to locate him and simply assumed he's been hiding among the guests."

The captain's spines stand straight up around his head and shoulders. "Why was this not reported immediately?"

"With everything else going on, we—"

"I don't want excuses." The captain slices a pincered hand through the air. He steps close to the cruise director and mutters, "Put this ship on security lockdown and verify the identity of every person on board immediately."

"Yes, sir." The cruise director scurries off, and crew members clear the riled-up crowd from the bay.

Tamara loops one arm through mine, pressing herself close. "What's going on?"

I grip her back, barely able to breathe. "Why would one of the crew hide among the guests? Are you suggesting he's some sort of serial killer?"

"I'd be surprised if he means her any harm," the captain says, but his spines are now laying flat against his head in a way that makes me think of a dog that's afraid of getting beaten. "Let's wait and see if they're just holed up somewhere on board."

Kiozhi clears his throat. "How many ships have docked with the *Romantasy* since she disappeared? Humans are big business on the black market."

My knees threaten to give out. I don't know if the black market is better or worse than being murdered by a serial killer. "You think that's what happened to her?"

"I don't know," he says, his face somber. "But we won't stop searching until we have her back."

"I've ordered the latest bio-scanners from my company," Nazhin says. "They should be here soon to help search the ship."

Kiozhi opens his ICC. "I'll reach out to my contacts at the shipping hubs and have them keep their eyes open for any unusual traffic."

"Great idea," says Tazhio. "I can do the same with friends in the shipping lanes."

"Thank you." I take my sister's hands. The same the terror gripping my heart is reflected in their eyes. With more conviction than I feel, I say, "We're going to find her."

"And she's going to be fine." Jennifer lifts her chin. "Out of all of us, Bethany is the most stubborn, most determined, and the most likely to survive despite the odds."

Tamara adds, "If anyone will be okay, she will."

I smile tightly. "Damn straight."

I thought that escaping the planet meant we were finally safe, but it seems our tribulations aren't over yet.

ear Reader,

I hope you enjoyed visiting (and escaping!) the Singing Planet with Suzanne and Kiozhi. But how horrible to come home and find out baby sister Bethany is missing! We'll wrap up the cruise by finding out what happened to her and her grumpy chef in the next book, Izhima

An alien cook convinces a snooty human with amnesia that she's his mate. How long can he keep up the charade before everyone discovers the truth?

Until next time!
Love, Tamsin

IZHIMA

SNEAK PEEK

IZHIMA

I look with dismay at the long list of recipes for "gluten free birthday cake" listed in the database from Earth's world wide web. When the steward asked me to make it, I assumed "gluten free" was a flavor and that I'd be able to easily find a recipe. But apparently there are additional options like chocolate, white, lemon, vegan... the list goes on and on. Even the article titled "Best" has over twenty variations.

"This would be so much easier if I could talk to the client in person," I grumble. The *Romantasy's* crew members are only permitted to interact with cruise ship guests on an as-needed basis; I guess baking a special order item isn't considered "needed." Not that I'm great with people, but sometimes it's required.

I tap my fingers against the burnished metal countertop in time to the music playing on my ICC. Though I've never met someone from Earth and am not likely to on this voyage, my matrix is currently in human form. I always assume the form of the species I'm cooking for; it helps me better understand their culinary methods. And regardless of how unimportant the cruise director believes this special order to be, I'm going to give it my all. One of the judges for the Nebula

Chef awards is on board, and I want to earn the first ever Nebula Star for Earth cuisine.

A recipe for something called a classic bundt pops up; the shape reminds me of a Hypawan cuttlefish. I pause, considering. Should I go with classic or unique? If I choose something simple and classic, I have to get it absolutely perfect. But the judge is likely to grant more leeway on something challenging. Pursing my lips, I continue scrolling.

I have the kitchen to myself, and only half the lights are on. Utensils hang from racks above the island counter in the center, and burnished metal and heat-resistant glass fixtures surround the edges of the room. This area is officially closed for renovations, but other than a warning posted next to the garbage evacuation button, the kitchen is fully functional. I'll have to clean up after myself and haul any waste out by hand, but the privacy is worth it.

A recipe for cake doughnuts scrolls past, then something called a funnel cake. Both use a technique called "deep frying," which is basically boiling in oil. According to the servers I've spoken with, humans on the cruise have a preference for such foods, and the funnel cake looks like it will stack nicely between layers of frosting.

I shrug. Why not? I can spend all night scrolling through options, or I can make a test cake. If the results aren't satisfactory, I have time to start again.

Turning up my music, I start assembling the ingredients.

I grip the stem of a glass holding a mildly alcoholic beverage in one hand while I hover near the service elevator set into the floor of the *Romantasy's* observation deck. The strange spicy scents coming from the nearby hors d'oeuvres tables would usually intrigue me, but tonight I need to stay focused. My entire career could hinge on this slightly underhanded scheme, but it's not like I have a lot of other options.

Overhead, the domed ceiling reveals a glowing yellow planet surrounded by multi-colored rings, while an alien orchestra plays a lively tune from a circular stage in the middle of the room. Nearby on the dance floor, I catch the familiar laugh of my oldest sister, Suzanne, as she waltzes by in the arms of a blue-skinned alien. At least she's having fun. I've lost track of my other two sisters, but I'm sure they're here, too; we're required to attend these nightly meat-markets as part of our free cruise package.

A winged alien with five short horns sprouting from his forehead catches my eye and angles toward me, but I level my best resting bitch face in his direction until he changes course. I probably should've opted for something less sexy than my elegant black evening dress and stilettos, but there's a chance I'll be on camera this evening, and I need to look my best.

I'm not on this cruise to have fun. My primary focus is the food—more specifically, the chefs. Two weeks ago, my producer threatened to cancel my baking show if I didn't come up with a plan to improve ratings.

I was at a loss about what to do until my sister won tickets to this luxury space cruise. Aliens are all the rage since the galactic prince married a human last year, and hosting a real-life alien chef on my show could send ratings sky-high.

Yet here I am, three days in, and I have yet to even meet a chef in person. Apparently, the Intergalactic Dating Agency has a policy against staff mingling with guests, and no matter how much I protested, pleaded, or pouted, the cruise director refused my request. Everyone acts like I intend to jump the chef's bones on sight or something. The best I could do was commission the a chef named Izhima to bake my birthday cake as an audition.

I study the food spread across the table again. At least my producer will be impressed by the guy's Nebula

Chef credentials. My birthday is tomorrow, and I've used a sizable portion of the show's marketing budget to book one of the ship's small restaurants for my party. I even pulled a few strings to invite the galactic crown prince, Arazhi and his new bride, Georgie. Go big or go home, right?

But the show is about more than just the food—the guests need camera appeal, and the only way to prove that is to capture Chef Izhima on camera. Hence, my current somewhat nefarious plan to be smuggled into the kitchen. The steward I bribed cost almost as much as the restaurant booking, but if I can get a few shots around the kitchen and a couple of angles with the chef at work, it will be worth it. Once I have those pieces, I can focus the rest of the footage on the show stopping presentation and taste test. I can't afford to let this plan go sideways or I'll lose the show for sure. And I am not a loser.

I bite my lip and look around the vast, crowded room. Where is my contact? I've been standing here since the party began. It's impossible for him to miss me.

I check the clock on my phone for the tenth time in as many minutes. I paid in advance, so that little alien better not stand me up. Though if he does, I'm uncertain I can tell one short gray alien from another to ream him out…

The elevator cycles open for what feels like the hundredth time tonight and my pulse quickens. A thin gray alien wearing a white crew uniform rises into view. He looks like he comes straight out of the Roswell picture books, with an oversized head and huge dark eyes, and he hurries straight toward me. *Finally.*

"Are you ready, miss?" The alien looks from side to side nervously. "The corridor will be vacant for a short span of time while the servers ready the next courses. We must be quick."

"Not a problem," I say and follow him to the circle on the floor. The lift descends with dizzying speed, making my already nervous stomach lurch. I'm still reeling as we come to a stop in the middle of a corridor intersection.

"This way." My escort hurries down the passage. Unlike the ornately decorated guest areas of the ship, the walls and ceiling of this wide corridor are a featureless gray, though the deck is painted with symbols I can't decipher. If I didn't have the alien leading me, I'd be utterly lost down here. I pause to snap a photo of the symbol on the floor so I can get back on my own if I need to.

When I look back up, the alien is already several yards away. I run to catch up, my stilettos clicking against the hard deck. Ahead, the familiar bustle and clank of working kitchen staff echoes from an open hatch on the left. We slow as we approach, and my guide says, "We need to pass by here quickly." He peers around the corner, then beckons to me and whispers, "They're not looking. Hurry."

I tap record on my camera and aim it inside as I scurry past, barely daring to breathe. Three or four alien cooks move around stainless-steel counters, too focused on their work to notice us. I'll take a better look at what I filmed them doing when this is all over. Maybe I can work some of it into the demo.

We turn down another hall, moving past hovering carts of neatly folded linen before coming to a stop at a closed hatch. The small alien gestures toward it. "Chef Izhima is in here."

I hand him several of the credit chips we used on board as tips, thinking it might be good to reinforce the bribe. "Thank you."

The gray alien grins, small mouth displaying what looks like glistening gray gums instead of teeth, and presses the door control. "Have fun."

As the door shushes quietly open, music emerges from inside, a woman singing in a language I can't understand. My alien escort scurries away.

I grimace. Guess I'm on my own to get out of here. *Good thing I took photos of the floor symbols.*

Taking a steadying breath, I start recording and slip into a half-lit kitchen.

I squeeze another artful loop of green frosting onto the stack of golden brown funnel cakes when the sound of someone clearing their throat draws my attention.

Annoyed by the interruption, I glance over my shoulder. A human with auburn hair pulled away from her pale skinned cheeks stands just behind me. She wears a black dress that hugs the curve of her waist and is slit to expose a considerable portion of her thigh. My heart cramps in my chest, and I suddenly understand why the humans have been kept from us. If I wasn't currently consumed by my project, I might be tempted to flirt.

Instead, I say, "You're not supposed to be in here."

"I'll leave in a minute." Her pink lips spread in a winsome smile that makes my groin tighten. "I only need a few seconds of footage."

My eyes narrow. The cruise director told me the human who ordered the cake is some sort of video celebrity on her planet. I glance at the order on my ICC to read the words I'm supposed to scrawl across the surface of the completed cake. "Are you Bethany Bloom?"

"That's me." Her bright smile falls as her gaze drifts to the stack of funnel cakes I've assembled. Though the confection isn't complete, I'm proud of how it is coming along. The whipped green frosting I concocted has a perfect balance of rich and sweet that won't overpower the delicate flavor of the cakes.

"Is that... my cake?" she asks, her voice hoarse. She's staring at it as if it's a delivery of three-day-old fish.

My *Iki'i* is sensing dismay from her, and I don't understand why. I set the piping bag aside and turn to face her fully. "Is this not what you expected?"

"Absolutely not. Where did you find the recipe for this... this... whatever this is?" Her fury feels like a flame thrower against my *Iki'i*.

My own indignation rises. Perhaps I was wrong about why the crew is shielded from the human guests. This female is quite abrasive. I lift my chin. "I searched our database on human cake extensively to formulate this recipe. This will please the human desire for both fat and sugar."

"Oh, my God. You have no idea what you're doing. We have to start over." She strides across the kitchen as if she owns it.

"Now hold on—"

"We need to fix this. Fast." She glances around, veering toward the far wall. "I need butter, eggs, sugar, flour—"

I grab her arm, my irritation barely in check. "You can't be in here, Beth. Just tell me what's wrong and I'll fix it."

She jerks away, her brown eyes flashing. "It's Bethany, not Beth. And you can't salvage this thing. All of it's wrong. I'm not leaving this up to chance again. I can show you how to whip this up in a few minutes, and once it's baking, I'll leave."

She's annoyingly resolute. Before I can stop her, she reaches up and hits the button for the garbage chute.

I barely have time to take a breath before the door irises open and a hurricane of wind and flying utensils sweep through the kitchen. Normally, the chute opens to a repository that is ejected through a secondary airlock—which is apparently open. We're swept out into space with the rest of the kitchen's contents.

The sudden silence is startling, and I harden my matrix to protect me against the vacuum of space. But then I see Bethany spinning next to me, her face a mask of terror. The whites of her eyes are turning red, and crystals of frost are creeping across her skin.

Kuzara. She's a pain in the ass, but I can't just abandon her. She'll be dead in mere moments. I stretch out a hand and pull her against me, encapsulating her in my matrix before hardening again. I've just cut my survival time down exponentially, but I've more than doubled hers. On my own, I can survive space quite a while in a state of hibernation, but maintaining oxygen and warmth for her will drain me quickly. I can only pray someone on board the *Romantasy* notices what happened before it's too late.

This damn female is going to be the death of both of us.

PREORDER IZHIMA to have your copy delivered straight to your reader on release day!

GLOSSARY

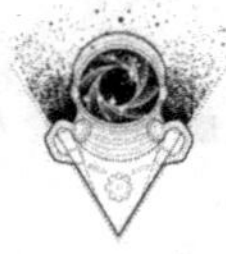

Bacca - a game that resembles frisbee golf.

Bareshi - brilliant one.

Burendo - a Kirenai who excels at shapeshifting and is able to not only assume the form of other species, but coloration as well.

Fogarian - aliens with red hair and sideburns who live on a rocky, mountainous planet.

G'nax - a species that uses light to communicate attraction and arousal. They also have a symbiotic relationship with an eight-legged insectoid.

Hage - bald, wide-eyed alien that looks much like the iconic alien humans have circulated.

Happa trees - blue fronds resembling palms.

Hypawa - species with magma colored eyes.

ICC - Integrated Circuit Chip - an embedded chip that is an alien version of a holographic smart phone

Ijin'en - four legged herd animal raised for meat and well known for its stupidity.

Iki'i - empathic power.

Irn - a unit of measure. One planetary rotation around the Kirenai's sun.

Jiro - a unit of measure equivalent to approximately two Earth hours.

K'ogai - the town near the palace on Kirenai Prime.

Kazhitu - nuts that look like sticky buns when baked. High in sugar, buttery and fruity.

Khargals - gray horned aliens with stone-like skin and wings from the planet Duras ;)

Khensei - a toxin that causes Kirenai to denature into their resting state.

Kikajiru - my distracting one - a term of endearment.

Kirenai Prime - the Kirenai home planet. Purple and blue with swirling white clouds.

Kuzara - shit, damn, fuck.

Kryillian death swarm - tiny insectoid creatures that can kill a man within seconds by sucking his blood.

Lensoran bubbly - alien champagne

Lonala moth - fragile insect native to Hypawa

Malila flowers - fragrant, night-blooming flowers popular in conservatories across the galaxy

Matrix/cellular matrix - the term for a Kirenai's cellular mass.

Nilgawood - a tree used to make resin.

Oritsu - An expression of awe.

Popotan - the plant used to line ship interiors that provides oxygen, recycles water, is highly resistant to radiation, and can regenerate itself if damaged.

Qalqan - a species known for their healers. Good bedside manners due to their resistance to emotional fluctuation.

Resting state - a Kirenai's amorphous shape, like nakedness to humans, it is shown only to family or trusted friends.

Senburu - a galactic conglomeration of merchants who oppose the emperor's rule. Individual members are called *Senbur.*

Sireta Prime - a popular party planet.

Sowain - tastes like chicken!

Supo cloth - smart fabric for clothing that doesn't need buttons or zippers.

Teozhisa - a cart to carry people.

Tolonovone - a device that creates lighted markings on the skin. Used by G'naxians as part of their mating rituals.

Ukimi ice - beloved dessert with cool, spicy flavor like sweet mint.

Urru - purple egg-sized fruits from the Singing Planet that taste like cantaloupe

Vatosangans - species with alabaster skin and blue or green hair who tend to be stocky or rounded. Planet is called Vatosang.

Kirenai are an all-male species of shapeshifters with a natural form (resting state) like an amoeba who usually assume a bipedal shape to interact with other species. Until the discovery of humans, Kirenai required a permanent pair-bond with a female of another species to produce offspring. All Kirenai traits are dominant and located on the Y chromosome; male offspring are fully Kirenai, while female offspring are fully of the mother's species.

Birth rates have been historically low, and over the ages, the population has dwindled. Human females are exceptionally receptive to impregnation, and do not require formation of a pair-bond to conceive, which has made Earth a target for black market slave traders who deal in "breeders." The Emperor is making attempts to protect the population.

Regardless of the shape a Kirenai's matrix is in, he cannot change his skin or hair color. The most common color is blue, although hues range anywhere from mint green to lavender. Rare individuals, called *burendo*, can vary coloration outside this range. Kirenai blood is clear or slightly milky unless infected, when it grows murky to almost solid white.

All Kirenai have empathic abilities called *Iki'i* which make them capable of reading emotion and desire, and also enables them to identify individuals within their own species regardless of shape. This is the only Kirenai trait sometimes passed on to female progeny. The ability also makes the species consummate lovers because they can take actions and form attributes their partner finds most appealing. Bonded mates assume a permanent form pleasing to their mates; rarely can they force themselves into an alternate shape after bonding.

The average Kirenai life-span is approximately eight hundred human years. When a pair-bond is formed, a Kirenai passes a small genetic market to his mate that mitigates the aging process, giving the mate a lifespan to match his own.

OTHER GALACTIC RACES

Qalqan – A pink, lizard-like race who are innately skilled at medicine. They have more than two genders and change genders as they age, which makes reproduction rather complex. It also means means they rarely pair-bond with Kirenai. In addition, their emotions are hard to understand for others and unreadable by Kirenai *iki'i*.

Hypawa – A race with large, expressive eyes, smooth luminescent skin, and luscious hair on their heads and eyelashes; considered by many to be the most beautiful race in the galaxy. Their origin is a mystery - even their supposed world of origin doesn't seem to be their homeworld. Their economy is dependent on tourism and entertainment.

G'nax – A spiny, bug-like race that can breathe a variety of atmospheres. Biologically they are inclined to be traders and have senses that let them navigate through hyperspace. They use light to communicate attraction and arousal. The females have a symbiotic relationship with an eight-legged insectoid which secretes dew used to feed G'naxian infants.

Khargal – A horned, gray-skinned race that can enter a hybernating state where their body becomes stonelike. The number of horns indicates the amount of royal blood in them. Honor is more important to them than anything. They have wings and claws and resemble gargoyles of Earth mythology. Their planet of origin is a barren world that has two moons and is known for having some unusual ore deposits and relatively few life forms.

Fogarian – A burly, thick-skinned race with crimson hair, claws, and fangs. They come from a high-gravity planet rich in crystalline gemstones and excel at digging. The females usually bear litters of two to four offspring, and are favored mates for Kirenai. Fogarians tend to be very straightforward and keep their promises, even if it means death.

Vatosangan – A small, slight race with alabaster skin, rounded features, and blue to black hair. As the most common race to pair-bond with Kirenai, some say they actually control the galactic empire behind the scenes. They seek any alliance, technology, or advantage that will benefit them, and their current government is a meritocracy.

Klen – A green-skinned humanoid race with eyes on extendable stalks. Their tongues can act as prehensile limbs, and they have the ability to withstand a wide range of temperatures. They are a race of scavengers and can modify some of their bodily secretions to become various useful substances.

Hage – Short, bald, gray-skinned aliens with large heads. They were the first to make contact with humans. Though their scrawny frame doesn't suggest it, they are addicted to the pleasures of taking nutrition, and their cuisine is spectacular. A past war obliterated their homeworld, and they now live scattered among the other races, usually employed in a service capacity.

Sheeghr – Not advanced enough to be admitted to the Galactic Confederation. A matriarchal, ferret-like race native to the Singing Planet. Known for hypersexuality, the females maintain a constant state of pregnancy to ward off a native parasite called a Gloor. Any female who refuses or who cannot get pregnant is killed. The males determine rank based on the size and color of their phalluses.

Human – New members the Galactic Confederation. This bipedal race has not yet homogenized into a single language, culture or appearance. The species has skin tones that vary between black and alabaster, with shades of brown in between. The females are capable of reproducing with many other species throughout the galaxy, and have become a target for illegal slave trading.

INTERGALACTIC DATING AGENCY

Looking for more out of this world romance? Your local Intergalactic Dating Agency can help! These strong, smart, sexy aliens are on the prowl for mates, and humans like you are exactly what they're after. Jump in with Book 1 of any standalone trilogy from our crew of rock star SFR authors and make steamy first contact! Warning: abductions may or may not be included!

Grab more hunky alien action here:

http://romancingthealien.com

<u>**Kirenai Fated Mates (Intergalactic Dating Agency)**</u>

Arazhi

Zhiruto

Iroth

Tazhio

Nazhin

Kiozhi

Izhima

****POST-APOCALYPTIC SCIENCE FICTION WRITTEN
AS TAM LINSEY****

Botanicaust

The Reaping Room

Doomseeds

Amarantox

9 781950 027668